LUCKY IN LOVE

A SUMMER BRIDE DUET

MATILDA MARTEL

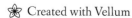 Created with Vellum

For my sisters

AGREEABLY ARRANGED

AGREEABLY
Arranged

A SUMMER BRIDE DUET, BOOK 1
MATILDA MARTEL

ONE

CASTOR

"Absolutely, not. I'm not considering this for a second." I'm emphatic, brash and as direct as I can possibly be, but I get the impression neither of my parents are listening to a word I'm saying. Only minutes have passed since I informed them of my appointment, an incredible opportunity, years ahead of schedule, and the only thing they can utter in response is suggestions for wives.

"I was thinking of one of the Lennox twins. They're pretty girls. What do you think, Castor? Delilah? Diandra? Which one do you prefer?"

My mother stares at me, waiting for my reply. She's done this since I was a child. Whenever I say anything that she disagrees with, she pretends not to have heard a word I said. When I told her, it was my intention to attend Stanford and not Harvard, the family alma mater, she ignored me and instructed the butler to throw every piece of correspondence with a Palo Alto address into the trash. She then forged my signature and applied to Harvard for me.

I've been infinitely fortunate to have grown up with every luxury imaginable, but there has always been a cost. Separately, Viola and Kenneth DeWitt are intolerable, insufferable people, but together, they are and have always been, a nightmare.

"Did you not hear me?" I pour myself another drink and glare at the pair while they scribble some notes.

"We heard. We're just not listening to you. This nonsense has gone on long enough, Castor. You turn thirty-five this year. We let you do this your way, and you have failed miserably."

My father stands to stress his vexation. "You will marry, and you will marry someone suitable before the end of summer or we are cutting you off and leaving everything to your younger brother."

"Didn't you cut him off already?" I bark, sitting confidently across from them.

"That can be altered. He's married now and working on getting his life together. To our surprise, Lucius found someone from a good family, which is more than I can say for you. You're thity-four-years old, people say you're a philanderer and worse, some assume you might be gay." He takes a strong sip, as if the word has tainted his lips.

He's such a jackass.

"Well, which is it? Am I a philanderer or am I gay? Or am I a gay philanderer?"

I scowl sarcastically from my place on the opposite side of the room, furious but attempting to look as calm as possible. It isn't easy. They've lost their minds believing I would consent to an arranged marriage.

"This is all a huge joke, isn't it, young man? It won't be a joke when your brother inherits everything, and you need to learn to live within your diplomatic paycheck." My mother interjects, walking towards me to bring me back into their web.

Clenching my jaw, I fight the urge not to tell them both to go to hell and leave whatever they want to that sycophantic, pill-popping, drunk, but after everything I've had to endure throughout my childhood and into my thirty-fourth year, half a billion dollars feels like too much to throw away.

Exhaling with defeat, I sit down and observe them carefully. They will not let this go. After everything I've accomplished. I've given the last ten years to the foreign service, living most of those years abroad, biding my time in smaller embassies just for the opportunity, experience and hope of one day reaching chief of mission and for what? *For this?* The only thing they care about is that I'm unmarried. They have yet to congratulate me for being named Ambassador to France.

These marriages are just for show anyway, right? Everyone winds up having an open marriage, don't they?

I take a long sip of whiskey. "Not the Lennox twins. They're both intolerable to be around for over five minutes." This is undeniably true. I've never cared for either of them. Besides, there's no way I'll make this easy for them.

"Fine. At least we're getting somewhere. What about the Caulfield girl, what's her name?" My mother hums as she tries to recall the name of the most unattractive girl I have ever met.

"Heidi? No! I'd rather surrender my inheritance and turn over my money to Lucius now." I stand to leave but they call me back and promise to be more discriminating.

"There's that Wilder girl. Jane? No, Janet. She's a nice girl." My father's suggestion turns my stomach and I suggest we end this immediately.

"What's wrong with her?"

"She's 4'10 and looks like she's fourteen-years-old! She's repugnant. If these will be the women you offer, then leave me alone and let me find a wife in Paris." I growl with anger, but my suggestion makes them both recoil in terror.

"This is precisely what we are trying to avoid. You will marry someone before you leave. We don't want you to wind up like your cousin who married that woman from his time in St. Petersburg." My arrogant mother clutches her chest as if the prospect of me following in his footsteps would lead to her untimely death.

"You two are unbelievable snobs."

"Call us what you like, just don't humiliate us." My father leads us into the dining room, and I think about what I'll be giving up for that money.

Although I've never been a hopeless romantic, I did once believe I would find myself in a better marriage than my parents. I thought I would marry for love. Some of my friends are resigned to having their families push their future wives on them. They've known since puberty who they would probably marry and long ago made the decision that the money was more important than their freedom to choose the woman they love.

Their parents had arranged marriages. Their grandparents, and so on. Money, social status and prominence are a commodity. Marriages are a way to keep all three together with only the *best* families.

This mind-numbing process continues well into dinner. Every woman I have ever known, unmarried and even some newly divorced is brought up as a marriage choice. No one is appealing, not even remotely. Why didn't I find someone on my own? Why didn't I chase those stars?

I should have tried asking her out. She might have said yes.

"What about the Forsythe's? Yes, the Forsythe's have two daughters. What's the prettier one's name?" My father's suggestion quickly catches my attention.

"Lola? Lola Forsythe?" My pulse quickens and I fear showing too much excitement. Lola is perfect. I'll marry Lola. I'll marry Lola, now. *Tonight.*

I'll die a happy man married to Lola Forsythe.

"No, not Lola! She's just a child. I'm sure Elmer Forsythe will want to marry off his eldest daughter, first. She's a beautiful girl. You can't deny that, and the Forsythe's have generations of family in politics. You could use their connections."

My mother frowns, but I'm not pleased with this switch. If I'm agreeing to their sham marriage, the least they can do is give me the sister I want.

Besides, my Lola is far lovelier than that pain-in-the-ass Luna.

"Not Luna. She's incredibly disagreeable. I've never liked her. And Lola is twenty-years-old, she's not a child." I polish off my drink and stay firm.

"Lola is about to become engaged to Orson De Clare. I heard it from Lucius. You'll marry Luna and that's final. You've said no to everyone else."

My father digs into his meal. He's convinced himself his idle threats will scare me into complete submission.

But fuck him. Fuck Luna. And most of all, fuck Orson De Clare.

TWO

LOLA

"Are you seriously agreeing to this?" My sister Luna stares wild-eyed into the distance as she attempts to process this information. I wait before I tell her the rest. She doesn't understand Daddy expects the same from her.

"It's not what you think. No, sorry, it is what you think. Mommy and Daddy were arranged, too...sort of. It's not like they didn't know each other before they married. They had choices. They just had limited options. It's the same for us." I take a sip of my drink and sigh.

"Us? Watch your mouth, little sister! They can go to hell before they drag me into their fucked-up little schemes." She sneers, just as I expected. As anyone would expect. Luna's reputation as a rabid contrarian is legendary.

Orson's handsome and sweet. I could do much worse on my own. I'm sure I would. As Mother likes to remind me, I have no talent for picking thoroughbreds. And what difference does it make? There's no one good left in New York. No one stays faithful. No one falls in love. At least not in the company we keep. These are all business transactions and brokered arrangements to keep up appearances. Luna has always been popular in our circles and since she's four years older than me, I'm sure Daddy is picking someone important for her.

"Daddy says we're broke. He's not paying for my school or our place anymore and we'll be cut off if we don't go along. But I'm sure you can talk your way out of it. You're much more rebellious than I've ever been." I tease, trying to make light of an awkward conversation.

"But why Orson? Why not let you choose? So many men like you, Lola. I wonder what Daddy is getting out of it." Luna rolls her eyes, unaware of what's in store for her.

I stop eating and think for a moment. "Daddy says it's a good alliance between us and the De Clare's. Orson's father will invest heavily in the family's hotel in Croton, if it's a joint-family venture. Orson and I had dinner the other night. He wants to move forward, but we have a few more dates scheduled to be sure. Daddy is pushing for me to agree as soon as possible, but for now he's happy I'm agreeable." I stab at my salad and avoid her disapproving gaze.

"Lola, you're beautiful. You're gorgeous. You can find someone on your own. Why would you let them choose your husband? You'll have men fighting over you. You're so young. What's the rush?"

She bangs on the table as she speaks, reeling with irritation. Luna has always been more of a mother than a big sister to me. When we were little girls, whenever she would argue with our snobby mother, she would often pack her bags and threaten to run away from home. But every time she did, she insisted I come with her, because *who would take care of me if she wasn't around?*

"Oh, Luna, you know me. I don't like anyone, anyway. I don't think I have it in me to fall in love." I shrug my shoulders and try hard to bury the ache in my heart.

"That's not true. You like Castor DeWitt. You've always liked Castor DeWitt." She glares at me, narrowing her eyes in judgement.

"Castor's gay." I pout and return to my salad.

"Castor is not gay. He's one of the biggest man whores in Manhattan. I have multiple friends who have had him and--"

For the sake of my broken heart, I cut her off.

"I don't need to hear about your slut friends, Luna!"

I wrinkle my nose, purse my lips and toss my fork on the table.

"He doesn't want me, so he might as well be gay. End of story."

"He's much older than you, Lola. He didn't want you because you were a teenager. Maybe he'll want you now. Word around town is Miss Lola Forsythe is looking damn fine these days."

She laughs and hands me back my fork.

I shake my head in defeat.

"I doubt it. He'll always see me as a little girl."

THREE

CASTOR

L ola Forsythe. Little Lola Forsythe. Look at you. All grown up.

I search through social media, scouring for information on her love life, hobbies, travels, anything that might give me an advantage over Orson. It's my nature to be prepared, and I don't want to leave anything to chance. For the past two days, I've stalked her online, looking through photos, reading through comments and above all, fighting the urge to contact her for a date.

No, I should wait. The plan is to wait.

It's best not to make any sudden moves that will tip off her parents. I've kept quiet about my plans to make my case for Lola over Luna. She's so pretty. She's always been stunning, but now that she's older and filled out, she looks good enough to eat. While I search through more photos, I find some swimsuit shots from her time in Mexico last spring.

You, naughty girl. Is that a tattoo?

My finger follows the line of her bikini bottoms, from her left to her right hip, stopping on a small swirl of ink near her pelvic bone. That must have hurt. Zooming in, I try to figure out what it is. Perhaps her initials, a flower, maybe the name of a pet? With the photo expanded, I can see the faint shadow of her nipples through her white bikini top and I suddenly feel my cock throb in my pants.

Clicking further, there's a photo of her sunning herself. Her thighs are slightly parted, and I imagine my hands parting them even more, relishing the softness of her skin and the musky scent of her pussy as I lick my way up, tugging at her suit with my teeth until I pull it down and feast on her wetness.

Shifting in my seat, I adjust my cock in my pants before taking it out and stroking it, letting it get harder in my hand while I gaze at more photos of Lola Forsythe in her white bikini. A few more clicks and my mind spins with visions of her long legs, supple breasts, and the cleft that sometimes appears in her crotch— the one I'm probably only imagining when I zoom in to ridiculous lengths. Sweating, stroking, panting, I focus on those big, blue eyes, picturing them looking up at me while I offer to cum on her tits or her mouth, fuck I don't care, wherever she wants. Pushing my laptop out of the way, I erupt with a growl, spilling over my hand and mumbling Lola's name under my breath.

In the shower, I beat off again, thinking about Lola's lips, picturing her giving me head, desperately trying to envision what she'll taste like when I finally spread those milky white thighs and bury my mouth in her sex for the first time.

Her parents need to agree. I'm far too worked up to walk away and there's no fucking way I'm marrying Luna. I need to see this through.

But what if she's not interested? I am much older than her. Orson isn't bad looking and younger than me. Maybe she's happy to be matched with him.

Oh, fuck Orson.

Looking through a few more photos before bed, I spy a short video I hadn't seen before. She's with a male friend, but he doesn't look like anyone I know. She's laughing as he tosses her into a swimming pool. Jumping in, he embraces and kisses her in the water, running his hands down her back and probably squeezing her ass under the water.

I don't know that for sure, but it's something I would do.

My pulse quickens with rage, jealousy, or a mixture of both. Whatever it is, it's an unfamiliar feeling that quickly consumes me. I've never been a territorial, possessive or jealous man. There seemed no point to it. Suddenly, this feels different. Perhaps, because I'm considering marrying her and that asshole has his hands all over my future wife. No, it's more than that. *I like her. I've always liked her.*

So many of the girls I grew up with are mean-spirited, social-climbing jerks who look down on anyone who doesn't run in their circle. *Not Lola.* She's always been kind, thoughtful and I've never once seen her put on airs. I always knew she'd grow up to be a knockout, but she's exceeded all my expectations.

Tomorrow is a big day. My father is meeting with Elmer Forsythe. I know him. He didn't decide on one of the Forsythe girls because he appreciates their beauty. I'm sure the snob in him admires their pedigree, but he must have something over him. If I know Kenneth Dewitt, he won't give him much of a choice. Expecting the worst, I've asked Luna to meet me for breakfast on an important matter concerning her sister. And to my surprise, she didn't say no.

Luna hates me as much as I hate her. Maybe, this is a good sign. Maybe she knows something useful.

FOUR

CASTOR

I expected her to arrive late, but the hostess recognizes me and tells me my guest is waiting. This piques my interest. Luna and I have hated one another ever since I briefly dated her friend, Melanie. It was a horrible three dates, and I only extended it to three because I made the mistake of sleeping with her on the first. I wasn't trying to lead her on. I was trying to give it a shot but the more comfortable she became the more the *real* Melanie emerged. And the *real* Melanie is an unapologetic snob.

Luna was a good and loyal friend to her, but she was an asshole to me. She felt I displayed a lack of chivalry by dumping her too quickly. When I refused to apologize for it or act the tiniest bit remorseful, she threw a drink in my face. Just thinking about it, makes my blood boil.

That little shit.

Approaching the booth, I catch her glaring at me, sipping a mimosa and tapping her fingers on the table. Sharpening my eyes with judgement, I slide into my seat and remove my jacket.

Clenching my teeth, I hold in my vitriol and choke on my anger. I need her to be as forthcoming as possible with whatever information she might want to reveal.

"I'm still not sorry about Melanie. I'm just going to say it now." Well, that didn't take long.

She shrugs. "Melanie's a dick. I knew it even then, but I had to show proper support for my friend."

My eyes glaze over with hate. "You're a real asshole, you know that?"

"Yeah, yeah, so everyone says. I know why you want to see me." She holds her finger up, pauses our conversation and politely asks the server for another drink.

"You do?"

"I think so." She nods. "I overheard my parents talk. That's why I wanted to see you. If you hadn't contacted me, I would have reached out to you."

Luna spills it.

My father must have dropped some heavy hints why he wants to meet today and as far as leverage, old Ken does not disappoint. After Elmer lost the bulk of his savings to a ponzi con artist, Dad lent him a cool twenty million to help him pay off creditors. That was more than a year ago and repayments have been slow. But if we're family, he might see fit to cut that in half and give him the next ten years to repay it.

"Are they implying that I'm only worth ten million?" Luna snipes.

"You are not even worth five. I would never marry you." I bark.

"Castor, I find you utterly repulsive. But I'm not worried about myself. This could devastate my Lola and push her further into Orson De Clare's clammy hands."

She peruses her menu and leaves me hanging. When she takes too long, I bang my hand on the table.

"What? Lola? Orson's hands! Over my dead body!" Rage and the thought of Orson's mitts all over my sweet girl fester in my thoughts. He's not getting my Lola.

She freezes and lowers her menu.

"Castor? Do you like my sister?"

I pause. I've never admitted my feelings to anyone. Luna is the last person I should trust. Lola's been in my heart for much longer than I had any right to even cast my eyes on her and one false move could take it all away from me. Why didn't I just ask her out before all of this? She turned eighteen two years ago. I should have just taken my shot. Why did I wait?

Because you're a fucking coward. Yes. Yes, I am.

Gazing up at Luna's frightened eyes, I detect nothing but concern.

Nodding, I duck my head and whisper the words. "I love Lola."

Without hesitation, her hand covers her mouth and her face brightens with glee. When tears threaten to form, she shouts out for the waitress.

"Ma'am! Another mimosa! Please!"

Turning back, she reaches out and takes both my hands in hers.

"My sister adores you! She's loved you ever since she was a little girl and you rescued her from that bully Candace Phillips at Evan Ander's Fourth of July picnic in the Hamptons, do you remember? It doesn't matter."

She waves me off.

"I remember."

"She's marrying Orson because she doesn't believe she'll ever love anyone but you. She also doesn't believe you'll ever see her as anything but an eight-year-old girl in that stars and stripes bathing suit." She sniffles and chokes on the words.

"I used to love seeing her in that bathing suit."

"It was pretty adorable." I smile, recalling her enormous, blue eyes, wet with tears and her small lip quivering with sadness until I fetched her a fresh lemonade and walked her back to Luna— who promptly marched across the lawn and beat the crap out of Candace.

"I'm ordering pancakes. We need to plan, Castor." She stops and stares at me for a moment.

"Wait, a minute. Are your intentions honorable? You want to marry her, right? Not just have a good time?"

"I just fucking said I love her! Of course, I want to marry her! Why do you think I'm here! I want my father to arrange me to her, not you!"

I grab my menu and look for something hardy, smiling inwardly.

My Lola loves me.

"Okay, I had to ask. She's my baby sister. She means the world to me. I swear to God, I'll fucking kill you if you hurt her."

FIVE

LOLA

This is a nightmare. No, this can't be happening. *Castor's mine!* It's not fair. I pace frantically across my bedroom floor and try to come up with something to delay this catastrophe.

Mr. Dewitt and Daddy are downstairs, and I heard it all. He's not taking no for an answer. Daddy can't say no. He owes him too much and there's no way to pay him back so much money in so little time.

But what about me? Why can't I take this bullet? *I was always meant to take this bullet for my family!*

Falling to the floor sobbing, crawling, reaching aimlessly for anything to wipe my tears as this rotten, expensive mascara stings my eyes, I clutch my breaking heart and try to keep it from tearing in two.

And where the hell is Luna!!!

"Lola! What are you doing?! Sweetheart!!" Luna throws open the door and rushes in.

I can hardly see her through my tears and smeared eyeliner, but I reach for her shirt and try to pull myself up.

"Luna! Daddy! You!!! Castor! No!!!" Wailing incoherently, I fall to the floor again, howling in pain.

"Sweetheart! I don't want him! I'm not accepting this bullshit arrangement. I wouldn't do that to you." She tries to hug me, but I push her away. I know it's not her fault, but I'm too heartbroken to see straight.

And what if he's in on this? What if he wants her? I'll die!

Maybe, I'll fake an injury. That might work. They'll call everything off for now and I can think of a plan. Nothing too painful. Maybe just a minor fall that I can exaggerate into a concussion. While I search the room for something to help me stage this tragic scene, our mother comes barging in.

"Unbelievable! Your father has lost his mind. He needs to put his foot down. The Dewitt's can't possibly expect Luna to marry that cad, Castor Dewitt. Everyone knows he's sowed his oats all over Manhattan. God only knows what he's done overseas." She sits down on the sofa as Luna and I glance at one another in confusion.

What the hell is she up to?

"Mother, will you excuse us? I need to speak to Lola in private." Luna never wastes words.

"Sweetheart, I'm trying to help." She walks over, but Luna stops her.

"No, never. You want something. Out with it. You're plotting and so are we. What do you want? There's no time to waste." My sister raises an eyebrow. She and our mother have spoken to one another this way for as far back as I can remember. Mother has the same relationship with Nana.

"Castor is not a good choice. Hugo Butler wants you to marry his son, Max and has offered to invest heavily in all the family hotels in exchange for your cooperation. We would be--" She's cut off mid-sentence by Luna's roaring laughter.

"No. I will never marry Max Butler. We went out on a date two years ago and it was one of the worst nights of my life. *Not a chance.* Never bring this up to me again."

Luna turns to me, shakes off her irritation, inhales deeply and tells me the most beautiful, wondrous thing I have ever heard in all my life.

"Sweetheart, Castor doesn't want me. He wants you. Castor wants to marry you." She smiles and leans in closer, sensing I'm too stunned to have heard it all.

"Lola Alexandra Forsythe, did you hear me? Castor Dewitt wants to marry you and he's coming here today to ask for you specifical-ly." She winks and shifts her eyes towards my mother whose mouth has fallen to the floor.

"Lola! You're engaged! You can't marry Castor!" Mother rushes over and tries to come between us.

I don't hear a word she says. I'm going to marry Castor Dewitt. Lola Forsythe Dewitt. Mrs. Lola Dewitt. Angels. I see angels. No. I see babies. Lots and lots of babies with gray-blue eyes and black hair chasing after me, calling me Mommy and asking me nuisance questions that sound like music to my ears.

Luna takes my hand and leads me into the bathroom to get cleaned up. She always carries extra makeup in her purse and after my fit, I can't possibly face Castor like this. Mother frantically follows us and tries to dissuade me from something that was written in the stars. I'm too giddy to listen.

As always, Luna speaks for me.

"Lola. You've already accepted Orson's proposal." Mother nervously harps, staring at me through the mirror.

I shake my head and Luna replies.

"No, you know she hasn't. You agreed she could give it a few more dates before she decided. She *has* decided." She takes out a small tube of mascara and hands it to me.

"You've got killer lashes, Lola. You don't even need mascara." She smiles and I stick my tongue out, too excited to deny it.

"Sweetheart be reasonable. If you back out, Mr. De Clare will take away his support." Our mother snatches my lip gloss as I try to re-apply, but Luna snatches it away from her.

"Stop that! Lola has loved Castor since she was eight-years-old. If he asks her to marry him, she will say yes!"

"If?!" I panic.

She hushes me. "He's asking, sweetheart." Leaning in, she whispers in my ear, "He told me he loves you."

My knees weaken and as I feel the ground beneath me falter, my doting sister catches me. The man I love, the man I've always loved...he loves me. Castor loves me. Clutching her shoulder, I tremble as my eyes fill with tears.

"Luna...how can I face him? I'll cry. Does he know I like him too?"

She nods. "I didn't elaborate, but it thrilled him knowing you think of him too."

Exasperated with our chit chat, our mother shouts her disapproval. "Luna! Stop encouraging her!

Shocked by her show of emotion, we crank our heads in her direction and attempt to hold in our laughter. Tired of her ruining one of the happiest moments of my life, I finally address her.

"Mother, there is nothing you can say that will make me say no to Castor. What are you thinking? Do you plan to disinherit me? Go right ahead. You said we're broke. The Dewitt's are filthy rich. I could care less about the money but be reasonable."

Luna interjects. "I'm not marrying him and I'm not marrying Max Butler. You might as well let Lola be happy and keep Kenneth Dewitt from putting the squeeze on Dad. He just wants Castor married. I don't think he cares which sister he winds up with."

Leaving her and her shattered nerves in my old bedroom, we head downstairs, giggling like little girls.

"I never took you for someone with balls. *Bravo.* Castor and I already planned this out this morning. Follow my lead. You'll know what to do." She winks and squeezes my hand, rushing off mysteriously.

When I look toward the bottom step, I see Castor. His navy suit is perfectly tailored to his long, lithe, statuesque frame. His dark hair doesn't touch the collar of the finely pressed dress shirt that peeks over his jacket. It's crisp and white, only a shade lighter than his pale skin. When he turns to the sound of our footsteps, his gorgeous steel-blue eyes, the same eyes I've pictured staring down at me while his huge cock splits me open, take me in, *take me all in*, and I nervously wonder if he's just read my mind.

"Lola..." He smiles at me and I'm certain a childish grin crosses my face.

"Hello, Castor." I sheepishly take two steps, extending my hand for him to shake. When he bends down to kiss it, my nipples tighten and I'm sure I flood my panties.

Goddamn, he smells good.

"You look stunning, Lola. I'm so happy you're here." His hand lingers over mine, and my stomach twists trying to decide if I should pull it away.

"I do? You are?" I refrain from asking any more. I don't want to set my expectations too high. Maybe, he won't ask me today. Before I have time to think too long on it, he speaks.

"This isn't my idea. I'm not here for Luna. I never agreed to this engagement." His eyes dart over towards his parents.

"Did Luna speak with you?" He tilts his head to gauge my reaction.

I nod. "She did."

A heavenly grin covers his gorgeous face but before he can say anything, my parents walk in and Luna pulls me away.

Making hushed kissing sounds, she chuckles softly. "You make a lovely couple, little sister."

I cower and cover my mouth demurely as we file into the living room.

"He's so beautiful." The butterflies in my stomach are fluttering so fast, I feel lighter than air.

Luna makes a face. "He just better let me make the first move. I don't want it getting around town that Castor rejected me before I said no."

I frown and pinch her side.

"Fine, I'll put on a good show! You know I love you."

SIX

CASTOR

This is awkward. We discussed our methods, but Luna has gone rogue and is giving everyone in the room her version of the silent treatment, which is not very silent. She's been grunting and nodding her replies, even to my parents who do not understand what is going on. Her father looks mortified, but I feel relieved that she's making this easier on me. Lola is flushed red, but I detect a hint of laughter in her eyes.

She's so lovely. I just want this to end. I need to be alone with her.

Staring at her tiny figure, so slender but perfectly voluptuous in all the right places, my palms sweat thinking about all the places I get to explore in the coming years.

Her long dark hair tumbles down in waves across her semi-bare shoulders, giving me a peek of her sun-kissed skin. I love that dress. It reminds me of something she might have worn over the white bikini from the photos I couldn't stop jacking off to last night. She hugs her arms, cold from this drafty room and I'm tempted to hand her my coat. I'd love to smell like her for the rest of the day.

There's no way I can let Orson have her. I don't think I can stomach him anywhere near her. Those eyes, those lips, that face, those breasts, I want them all. I want those legs wrapped around my hips when I fuck her into the morning, and I want to hear that sweet voice beg me for more. There's so much I want to do to this girl, and I don't think I can wait until our wedding.

I need her now. Okay, maybe not here, but soon.

"Luna, you're acting childish in front of our guests. We've discussed your options and..." Mr. Forsythe attempts to rein in his daughter's antics, but he's quickly interrupted, and all hell breaks loose.

"I am not acting childish! This is a ridiculous farce and I'm not taking part in it any longer. I'm not marrying this man. He's too old. He's got a horrible reputation as a womanizer and he and I could never stand one another's company for more than fifteen minutes." After thoroughly insulting me, Luna, a woman I have always found wholly unattractive and have never understood why others adore, jumps to her feet and tries to storm out of the room.

She apologized beforehand for future insults, but I never cleared calling me old. I'm ten years older than her.

"Luna, enough!" Her mother's shocked expression is full of remorse, but my mother does not appreciate having her eldest son insulted. We expected this and Viola never disappoints.

"Forsythe! How dare you allow your daughter to treat my son in this fashion. You told us she was agreeable to this arrangement. Castor is more than capable of finding a more suitable match than your immature daughter."

Mr. Forsythe would like to defend his daughter's honor, but words fail him. As Luna assured, he turns his wrath on her.

"Luna Elizabeth Forsythe, you are cut off. I am freezing all your accounts this very hour."

"Daddy! How can you force something like this on me and expect me to agree? Shouldn't I have choices? He's the first one you've offered. What about Lola? If this match is so important, why not offer him Lola?" Luna fights a smile, but her father's mouth gapes open in shock.

Seizing my chance, I spring to my feet.

"That's a wonderful idea. I'll marry Lola. She's always been my preference." I turn to gaze at Lola, whose bright, blue eyes have grown wide with excitement. When she bites her lip to hide a growing smile, I shout out what I'd wanted to say all along.

"Will you marry me, Lola?"

A multitude of gasps sound off across the room, except for Luna who breaks out in a silly smile.

Mr. Forsythe panics, tries to block his daughter's path and attempts to remind me she is no longer available. But before his stammered words can fully stumble out, Lola shouts back and rushes over.

"Yes! I'll marry you!"

After sliding across the floor straight into my embrace, we smile at each other, far happier than either of us of should be for an arranged marriage, and kiss.

Not open mouth. Not in front of our parents.

My parents are stunned but within seconds their shock turns to elation. Their only desire is that I marry someone suitable and Luna has forfeited their approval. Lola is a marvelous replacement that will prevent them from another exhausting search.

On the other hand, Lola's father looks furious.

SEVEN

LOLA

I don't hesitate. I probably should play a bit harder to get but I can't. I've loved Castor Dewitt ever since I was eight-years-old and he defended me from that evil witch Candace Phillips, who always thought she was the boss of me. When he checked on me thirty minutes later and brought me a fresh lemonade to replace the drink she spilled, my school girl heart exploded. And it's been his and his alone ever since.

My parents know nothing of fate and soul mates. This is my destiny.

"Lola, you're engaged." My father tries to come between us but fails to wrench our hands apart.

"No, I'm not. Nothing is official yet and you know it. What does it matter? If Castor is good enough for Luna, why can't I marry him? Are you insinuating he's an inappropriate choice? Is he unsuitable?"

Mrs. Viola Dewitt gasps and clutches her priceless pearls.

"Elmer Forsythe, is that what you're driving at? What is the issue?"

"Yes, pray tell, what is your problem with my son?" Mr. Dewitt chimes in.

My father stands in the middle of the living room with egg on his face and tries to retrace his steps.

"Nothing is wrong with Castor, of course. But he is almost twice Lola's age." My father is beside himself, scrambling to find the words while he continues to follow Castor and I around the living room, desperate to separate us.

"We're only fourteen years apart and I'm fine with the age difference."

I look over my shoulder at the Dewitt's.

"This turned out better than expected. Don't you agree?"

Mrs. Dewitt nods and reaches for my hand.

"Welcome to the family, my dear. You must come for dinner tonight. We have plans to discuss. Castor leaves for Paris in six weeks. We need to get invitations out yesterday!"

"Let's get photographs done tomorrow. I want this announced in the Times next Sunday. We'll pay extra." Mr. Dewitt barks his instructions while his wife takes notes. I have a feeling this wedding will be a breeze to plan.

My parents try to smile as my new in-laws surround me, and Luna darts over to give me a hug. Castor looks devilishly handsome as he shakes my father's hand and suggests a wedding date five weeks out, allowing us a brief honeymoon before he's due in Paris.

My mother is unmistakably peeved. I know that look, but she's too nervous to speak up. Something has backfired. I fear there is some-thing no one is telling us.

Unwilling to let them rain on my parade, I keep my distance from both. Surely, they'll want to speak to me alone at the first opportunity. They'll want me to take back my promise.

Unthinkable!

Leaning into Castor, I suggest we depart together. "My parents will ask me to break it off as soon as you leave."

I bury my face against his muscular chest, hiding within his jack-et's lapels and inhale the cologne that's been driving me crazy since he arrived.

He clutches my hand firmly.

"You're coming with me. We need to pick out your ring." Kissing me sweetly, he smiles.

"We're getting married, Lola."

I nod and squeal with enthusiasm, aware that I am relinquishing all power by showing my hand and not giving a damn.

"I know, Castor. We're getting married."

EIGHT

CASTOR

This morning I heard from Orson De Clare. He's irate that I've stolen his bride. *What nerve.* Nothing was official. He never proposed, and Lola wasn't wearing his ring. I got both done the same day.

This could cause problems down the line. His family is well-connected, and I've heard he and his father are in league with the Butler's holding something over her parent's head, but I don't care. *Lola is worth it.*

You don't know how good it feels knowing Lola and I are together. My lips are sore and chapped from kissing my girl for hours last night, never moving past first base, like two kids in high school. I feared my interest was one-sided. She's so much younger and I know what people say about me. I'd be lying if most of it wasn't well-deserved. But I've never truly been in love with anyone.

I can't believe this is what it was supposed to feel like all along. I thought there was something wrong with me.

For as far back as I can remember, I've avoided commitment. Until now. *Until Lola.* This is something I want. It's not about what my parents want. It's not about what's best for my career. For the first time in my life, all I want to do is to be with one woman, claim her, take care of her, come home to her, make love to her every night and start a family...

Holy shit, did I just say that?

No, it's true. Lola and I will be good for one another. I feel it. It's only been twelve hours and I'm going crazy needing to see her again. Reaching for my phone, I fire off a text to my lady.

How's my beautiful girl?

Hey, gorgeous man.

I can't stop thinking about you. Are you sure you're still marrying me?

You know I am. Are we still on for tonight?

You know we are. I'll pick you up at 7:00.

It's silly. Although I've known her since she was a little girl and I've watched her grow up, there is so much more about her that remains a mystery to me. *But that's fine.* I have the rest of our lives to find out. So far there isn't anything I've learned that doesn't absolutely fascinate me.

There's always been something about my Lola that makes me take pause, a strange feeling or emotion. For years, it was almost brotherly. She's a sweet girl and with all the vipers hanging about, I felt drawn to protect her. But then things changed for me.

Four years ago, just before I left for my new assignment in Japan, I attended the wedding of a mutual family friend. Lola was there, fresh off her debutante ball. It had been a few years since I'd seen her, and I couldn't believe my eyes. She was still a pretty, little thing but had grown even more beautiful. She was sixteen-years-old, sweet, fresh, bright-eyed, innocent but with the body of a woman. Everything about her body had changed. Her breasts were full, her waist sloped sharply, her legs were longer and her behind was so perfectly round it made you want to fall on your knees and sink your teeth into her supple flesh.

And then I came to my senses and realized I was lecherously eyeballing a sixteen-year-old girl.

Thankfully, I left for Tokyo two days later. But I never got Lola out of my mind. The Forsythe's are crazy if they think I'll wait three months to marry her. I know what they're doing. They're buying time to break us up. Orson's phone call today, threatening my father's company, and using his connection to the Butler's are all part of their plan. Fortunately, my parents are taking this reluctance as an affront on our family honor and they're pushing back on Elmer Forsythe.

Old Elmer better get his fucking checkbook out and remember there are seven zeroes in ten million.

If they think I'll hand her over like a commodity they can trade up, they're out of their mind. Now that I have her, no one is taking her away. I don't care what I need to do. Lola is mine. *We will marry in five weeks.* I promised her I wouldn't leave for France without her and I'm not breaking it.

I ARRIVE at the small apartment she shares with her sister fifteen minutes early. Luna answers the door and immediately apologizes.

"Sorry I called you old. I had to make it realistic. *Tantrum Luna* has a mind of her own." She smirks.

"As long as I get Lola, I'll forgive any of your insults." I nudge past her and smile when I see the flowers I sent, pink roses, on display in the foyer.

Appearing concerned, she jerks her head to summon me closer. "I'm telling you this because I love my sister and she's crazy about you, not because I think you're such a wonderful guy." She whispers and steps closer.

"Our parents were here. They're pushing her to call this off and marry Orson. Lola has never gone against our parent's wishes. If by some chance you have your doubts or you're not going to take this seriously, please don't lead her along. She could be disowned over you." She leads me into their living room and walks off to fetch her sister.

Before she gets far, I feel the need to address her concerns. Luna Forsythe has always been a pain-in-the-ass. I've never understood why half the men in Manhattan worship her, but I've always respected how much she loves her sister.

"I am serious about this. I didn't think I'd ever want to marry until there was a chance, I could marry her. *Lola is my person.* Does that make sense to you?"

She nods, then stops. "Maybe...in theory. I've never felt that before." She looks away, sadly.

"I hope that changes."

NINE

LOLA

"I'm sure you've heard terrible things about me, sweetheart, and I wont try to defend myself. But I want you to know, I'm not like that anymore." Castor's gray eyes shimmer against the candlelight as he reaches for my hand. This is not a subject I care to discuss, but now I have no choice.

"You don't owe me an explanation. What's in the past, is in the past. I only want to determine if you would like a real marriage or an arrangement. Emma Waters and Kimberly Kent, both whom entered something similar, appear to have open marriages. Is that what you want? I just want us to be honest with one another." I gaze at him, dreading he may want the latter.

"Open? No! God, no! The thought never entered my mind. I want us to have a real marriage, in every sense of the word. I'm crazy about you Lola. Please tell me that isn't what you want." He grips my hand tightly, knitting his brow and attempting to shake off the anger that has momentarily consumed him.

I lean in and shake my head. "It's not what I want. I don't think I can stand the thought of sharing you with anyone else. It would break my heart." Staring into those beautiful eyes, I remember all the nights I dreamt of this day, the day he and I might one day be together, and for a second I fear tears will form.

"You won't ever share me." He kisses my hand, holding it against his lips for what feels like minutes.

"And I promise you, I won't ever share you. Do you hear me, Lola?" His stern glare turns provocative as he releases my hand and runs his fingers up my forearm.

I nod and chew my lip, while my heart flutters and my pulse races. *He's so beautiful.* How can my parents believe for one moment I could call this off? I'd elope with him tonight, if he asked.

Ask me, Castor. I can be ready in thirty minutes.

We gaze into each other's eyes without speaking. His smoldering stare makes me weak and I try to think of something to say. But there's too much tension in the air, sexual tension that feels like it's about to explode. It's too soon to take this further, isn't it? This is our first official date. If I put out now, am I a skank?

But we're engaged. Surely, that changes the rules. Doesn't it?

I feel hot, flushed, bothered, and so incredibly horny. I've waited so long. All these years, when everyone else was having fun and screwing party boys left and right, I held out for this man. The man sitting across from me, undressing me with his eyes. I don't think I can wait much longer. This virginity needs to go. This flower needs watering. I need cock and only his will ever do. It's right here in front of me, probably big and hard under the table.

What the hell am I waiting for?

"Will either of you be ordering dessert?" The waiter breaks our eye contact, when he presents the dessert tray.

Castor shakes his head and I swallow hard, working up the nerve to say the nastiest thing I've ever said to a man.

"No, thank you. We're having our dessert at home."

WE CHOOSE HIS PLACE. Luna is home binge watching the latest season of her favorite series and she'll be up halfway into the night. Besides, I have a feeling I'm a screamer. If my sister hears me in a state of frenzied lust, I may have to kill myself or her, to save us from the embarrassment of facing each other the following morning.

He fidgets and fumbles as he tries to unlock his door. When it finally opens, he pushes us into the darkness and swings me around until the only thing I see is his chest, then his hands gripping my face before his lips crash into mine. The world disappears when our mouths meet, nothing matters but him. His warm breath and the touch of his soft lips soothe me, filling my senses, weakening what little restraint I have, until my breath catches, and I whimper with need.

Pulling away from me, he gazes down and smiles sweetly, kissing my nose and sighing as he holds me close.

"Are you sure, sweetheart? We can wait, if you're not sure."

I lunge forward and kiss him, aching for more, desperate for him to stop teasing me and make me his forever.

This is what I've always wanted. It can't happen soon enough.

Unbuttoning his shirt with one hand, my free hand tugs away his jacket and I'm so consumed with my task, I don't notice he's unzipped my dress and let it fall to the floor.

"Lola, I've wanted you for so long, honey. I love you." He pants as he lifts me off the ground and carries me towards his room. My kisses don't stop. He tastes so good and feels so warm---I can't make myself stop.

"Oh, Castor, I love you. I've always loved you. I saved myself for you." I don't mean to admit something like that, but I feel swept away in the moment and to my horror, he pulls away.

"You did?" His mouth falls open and tears of shame well in my eyes.

TEN

CASTOR

I know what I just heard, but I can't believe my ears. I'm not worthy of this. It's always been my biggest fantasy about Lola, but in the back of my mind, I always knew I didn't deserve it.

She looks distraught.

Oh, shit. She thinks I'm turned off.

Swooping in, I recapture her full lips and swallow her gasp with a deep, savage kiss. I feel wild with passion, hungry to make her mine. Claiming her mouth, I pour everything I have into coaxing, teasing, devouring those perfect lips, filling her mouth with my tongue and tasting her breath. *I could kiss her forever.*

Every moan and every sigh that falls from her lips, makes me crave her more. When I feel her tremble, I lower my head, pull her closer and smother her neck with kiss after kiss— taking what's mine. *What will always be mine.*

"I love you, Lola. I don't deserve you. How can you love me?" My heart clamors in my chest, beating wildly, as I bare my soul to her. I've never felt so vulnerable with a woman and yet, for the first time in my life, I know I can let go.

With Lola, I can let go.

Her eyes drip with tears and her pouty lip quivers as she stares at me, stunned by my admission. Caressing my face, she kisses me gently and whispers. "I think I was always meant to love you. I know I'll love no one else." She sniffles and the mere suggestion of her loving anyone else makes me shudder with disgust.

Shaking my head as I pull her closer, I agree with her. "No, you won't. You won't get to love anyone else." Kissing her, I unhook her bra and finally bring my greedy hands to cup her soft, supple breasts. Caressing each mound, I feel her nipples tighten in my fingers as she giggles into my ear.

"Why are you laughing? Am I tickling you?" I didn't think I was *that* out of practice.

"What about our babies?"

"What?"

"You said I can't love anyone else." She smirks as she wraps her long legs around my lap and stares me down. Her gorgeous breasts are heavy in my hands, while my cock is inches away from her pussy, I can't think straight.

Considering what she's asked, I tighten my grip on her waist and lower her on the bed. Staring down at her, I gaze into those big, blue eyes and wonder how many times I imagined this very moment, the night I'd hold her in my arms and make love to her for the first time. I never really thought this day would come and now that it's here, she's asking me to give her babies.

That's not really what she asked. You're deliberately projecting.

Brushing her dark hair off her face, I tease her taut nipples as my hands explore every inch of her glorious body. Trailing kisses, I swirl my tongue around a hard bud and listen to her sweet voice calling my name. She holds me closer, letting me suckle deeper, engulfing and tugging her sensitive flesh until she writhes and whimpers, urging me to continue. The smell of her skin and the heat radiating between us quickly overwhelms me. When I drop to her abdomen, I consider something I never thought to ask.

"Sweetheart, are you on the pill?" Licking and nibbling on her tight stomach, I grin from ear to ear. This is a combination of my top three Lola fantasies: marrying her, being her first and knocking her up. This is too much. I'm never this lucky. Lightning will surely strike me dead on this unbelievably clear night, while we make love.

She shakes her head. "No. Oh, no. Should we stop? This all happened so fast." She looks down as I inch my way towards her thighs.

I freeze. I don't want to stop, and I don't want to take precautions. If she wants to, we can and will, but we're getting married in five weeks. I'm up for some Russian Roulette, if she is.

"We don't have to, but we can."

Her expression softens. "I don't want to stop. We get married in five weeks, right?"

That's all I need. Spreading her legs, I take slow licks up her thighs, watching her whine, twist and pant, whimpering with anticipation. She's so wet, the poor thing has soaked her panties through, giving me a visual that will surely haunt me for days.

This is all too much. Licking the fabric, I taste her, and her musky scent invades my senses.

I feel like tearing these panties off with my teeth.

She reaches for them, desperate to give me access, trying to get them off, but I stop her.

"Let me, Lola...please, baby." Rising, I bring her legs together, and slide them off catching my first glimpse of her bare, puffy lips, drenched with honey I'm seconds from feasting on.

It's perfect and it's all fucking mine.

I can't stop myself. I don't even give her a chance to drop her legs. Swinging them open, I dive in, burying my mouth in her sex, stabbing her deep with my tongue and letting it slide up her slit. When I reach her clit, I feather it gently, observing her twitch and gasp, shuddering with every lick and surrendering to pleasure.

Feasting on her, devouring and suckling, I explore every bit of her pussy with my tongue, but keep coming back to her slit, stroking it, making her grow wetter and wetter until I'm drowning in her taste and seeking more by the second. When I push my fingers inside her, thrusting them into her sleek passage to send her over the top, she loses control. Her soft whimpers become screams as her back arches and her hips buck off the bed.

"Castor! I love you! You're making me come. I can't believe you're making me come." I relish her praise, watching her body spasm while the growing tension explodes and she convulses in ecstasy, only inches from my face.

It's stunning. She's stunning. And I'm about to come in my boxers. I'm only human.

Tugging roughly, they nearly rip when I yank them off my legs and toss them to the other side of the room. I'm so hard. I've been hard on and off since dinner and the build-up has only worsened since we arrived. I need to make love to her, and I can't wait a second more.

ELEVEN

LOLA

I watch him, those eyes, that body, he's coming for me and my heart is beating so fast, I just pray I don't die until after he's finished. My gaze travels down to the thick cock jetting out between his legs, and my mouth waters. It's perfect.

It's a little big and scary, but I can take it. I'm ready. I've been ready for years.

When he lowers his body over me, the feel of his weight thrills me. His warmth, his scent, the intensity of the moment, almost moves me to tears, but instead of crying, I shamelessly spread my legs wider and bring him closer, encasing him in my limbs.

"I love you, Lola." He croons and the words take my breath away.

He loves me. Castor Dewitt loves me.

"I love you. I've waited so long for you. I don't want this to end." I exhale deeply, feeling him position himself, ready to take me, ready to make us one. But he stops and gazes at me, brushing a few stray locks from my face.

"I've waited for you. Maybe I always knew there was something special about you, sweetheart. When that little girl pushed you and knocked the drink out of your hand, you looked at me with tears in your eyes and all I wanted to do was protect you and..."

Slamming my lips to his, I wrap my arms around his neck and burst with tears of joy. "Castor! You remember! You remember that day. You don't know what that means to me!"

Crying, gasping, panting, I instinctively circle my legs around his hips and bring mine up, searching for him, wanting him. I'm shameless and I don't care. I'm his, forever. Caught off guard, he thrusts into me, but he jerks back. Fearing he might have hurt me, he pauses, but the look of lust in my eyes puts him at ease.

I extend my arms, wanting him closer and he relaxes into me, taking my lips as his own. When he pushes into me, I feel him stretch me open, molding me to him, like I always knew he would, like only he ever will.

"Castor..." I whimper in pain, but I don't want him to stop. I never want him to stop.

"I'm sorry, baby. I think I'm hurting you." He kisses me and halts his progress but remains tightly sheathed within me.

"It's okay. Don't stop. I'll get used to you, please... Castor. I need you." I brace myself and he thrusts forward, shredding my innocence and filling me completely.

I gasp, bring my knees forward, and let him sink even deeper. Every move makes me whimper and moan for him. The pain is nothing compared to the pleasure. *I could die from this much pleasure.* I can't get enough of him, of us. When he pulls out and glides back in, repeating the motion, widening my walls, the pain becomes a sweet friction that makes my eyes go back in my head.

His beautiful gray-blue eyes find mine. Gazing provocatively as his cock barrels into me, he lifts my hips off the mattress and give me a pleasure I've never known. With every thrust, he silently asks for my surrender and I lose myself to him, willingly, enthusiastically.

This is all I've ever wanted.

Moaning, screaming for more, I feel my pussy flutter around his shaft, squeezing it and sending waves of ecstasy shattering through me. I'm unable to contain my volume. *I try but I can't.* Crying out, I whimper against his shoulder, clawing his skin, writhing against him, while wave after wave of savage desire seizes me, wracking my body into submission.

"Lola, I'm coming. You feel too good. I can't hold on." Castor grips my hands and thrusts harder, tumbling over the edge at full speed.

"Come inside me. Please." I beg, wanting to feel him, desperate for everything.

He claims my lips again, sweating, gasping for air and smiles. "Do you want me to give you a baby? Is that what you want?" He croons and I melt.

I nod. "Yes...please, more than anything."

"I'll give you whatever you want, Lola. Now and always." When our mouths meet and our tongues intertwine, I feel the vibrations in his growl as he finds his release, filling me with his seed.

I'm his and he's mine. Forever.

TWELVE

CASTOR

My father wants to see me, but I hate leaving Lola so early. She's spent almost every night with me for the past week and every minute away from her is torture.

"Don't worry, I need to get home, sweetheart. Luna and I are having a light breakfast before my fitting. You were so good to get my dress and I don't want to be late for my appointment. It's a simple thing, but they have to take in the hem." She smiles and sits up, giving me an incredible view of her breasts as she searches for her bra.

Spying it on the floor, I kick it further away, making her crawl out of bed and walk the few steps to retrieve it. The sight of her flawless body, formerly pristine and now thoroughly corrupted, possibly pregnant, makes my cock harden against my leg.

"I wish you'd gone with the more expensive one. I told you I'd get you whatever you wanted. We don't need anything from your family. You're my responsibility now, Lola Forsythe, soon to be Dewitt." I grasp her waist and yank her closer.

"That sounds divine, my love. I can't wait to be Lola Dewitt." She ducks her head, and strolls away, searching for her clothes. I know it bothers her, but she refuses to admit it.

Her parents are still pushing for her to marry Orson De Clare and refuse to participate in any of the wedding plans. When her father denied her money for a dress, I cut them out of the process and said we, she and I, because everything I have is hers, would pay for it all. Since then, my mother has corrected me and insisted on carrying the load. She never had daughters of her own. Taking Lola to choose a wedding dress was one of the biggest highlights of her life.

As she prepares to head out, I take her hand and pull her into my embrace. "Don't be sad, sweetheart. They're being jerks. In one month, we'll be married and how we got there won't matter."

She nods and kisses me, making me long to carry her back to bed and spend the rest of the day making love to her.

But Kenneth Dewitt does not like to be kept waiting.

"What the hell does that mean?" My eyes sharpen with anger as I listen to my father's story. He's almost as upset as I am.

"Calm down, Castor. This is just a small hiccup. For some reason, Hugo Butler is teaming up with Theo De Clare to put the squeeze on Elmer Forsythe. Lola marrying Orson--"

I cut him off. "Lola is not marrying Orson."

"Just hear me out. Lola marrying him was supposed to help, but now that she's marrying you, they're out to ruin him. Deliberately.

Spitefully. I could call back the money he owes me, but he doesn't have it and they'll ruin him anyway. Gossip around town is Lola is going to be disowned and possibly smeared. They can't disinherit her. They don't have anything to leave her or Luna. This is concerning for you."

He leans back and gauges my reaction, expecting anger. And he gets it. "Listen old man, you wanted to arrange me. You wanted me to marry a Forsythe and I'm doing it. I'm not abandoning Lola because you're concerned about me marrying a black sheep. As it happens, she might already be carrying your grandchild, so any delays in our wedding date will look far more embarrassing."

His smug expression alters. "Castor. Couldn't you keep your hands to yourself a bit longer?"

"No. No, I couldn't. *Have you seen her?* Besides, we love each other. This is a love match for us and since we're getting married in a month, we wanted to get started on our family right away." I knit my brow and wait for him to say something shitty. He surprises me.

"Fine. Your mother seems pleased with her and the addition of a grandchild will make her decade. I need you to reach out to Max Butler."

"No. I can't stand him." I sneer.

"Do it for your wife. He'll know why his father cares about the De Clares. Hugo never cares about anyone but his son and his company. Why does it matter to him who Orson marries?"

"I don't know him well enough to get that kind of information. But Luna does. Maybe she can find out."

THIRTEEN

LOLA

"It's so nice having breakfast with my little sister. I've hardly seen you all week!" Luna eyes me, grinning wickedly as she takes a sip of coffee.

"You dirty tramp." She giggles and I almost shoot orange juice out of my nose.

"Stop that!" I swat her with my napkin. "I'm engaged, now. And I need to take care of my man." I smile and watch her mouth gape open.

Leaning in, she whispers. "So, how is he? You better not be faking it! Make him earn that shit!"

I swat her again. "Lower your voice, psycho. He's wonderful. Better than all my fantasies...hold on, I'm getting a text."

Castor is in the restaurant, looking for me. Jumping out of my seat, I wave him down.

"Oh my God, can't he leave you alone for one morning?" Luna sulks and quiets down when he approaches.

"Sweetheart, you look beautiful. Hi, Luna. Sorry to interrupt your breakfast together, I need to ask Luna for a favor." He sits down and tells the waiter he won't be staying.

Castor glares at Luna. Whatever he needs to say, it won't come out easy. But if he came all this way and is bothering to ask, it must be important. Luna is impatient and gazes back and forth, first to me then to Castor.

"What the shit? Just say it." She snaps.

"Luna, when was the last time you spoke to Max Butler?" He exhales with relief, having finally spoken the name.

"Max Butler? Luna? Are they still trying to set you up with him?" I narrow my eyes with concern, watching her squirm in her seat.

"Why?" She squeaks. It's unlike her not to anger at the mention of his name.

"Were they trying to arrange you to him?" Castor takes my hand and kisses it. An odd move in the middle of this awkward conversation, but I take my kisses as they come.

Luna is speechless, but I answer for her. "They were. Our parents never had any intention of letting her say yes to you. Mother said Max Butler wanted to marry her. His father was going to invest a ton of money in Daddy's hotels. Have you seen him, Luna?"

She shrugs. "Just a little."

"What the hell does that mean? You said you hate him." I bang the table and she perks up.

"I have needs and you've been gone all week! Max has been texting like crazy. That night it stormed, he came over to keep me company and then came back the night after that. But one more night and I put an end to it, I swear."

Castor and I stare at one another in amazement. "Luna! You said you hate him! How do you get hot and bothered for someone you hate?"

She shrugs, again. "I never said I hated having sex with him. I don't know why he wants to marry me, but he does. His father is helping him make it happen. He doesn't give a fuck about Orson except they had a deal to try and make this happen. I guess they're friends."

"Why are you encouraging him? He's letting his father ruin your family over it. He's the reason your parents want to disown Lola." Castor barks at her, but I place my hand on his forearm, calming him down.

"They won't disown her. They don't have anything." She sits up straighter in her chair.

I shake my head. "Not disinherit, disown. Daddy won't give me away, and Mother won't help me plan. They won't send invitations out, Castor's mother had to. And she paid for my dress. They're paying for everything. No one is speaking to me. Except you. Unless I call this off."

Scratching her hair, she bows her head and a look of dread crosses her face. "I'm sorry. What do you need from me?"

I sigh. "I don't think there's any--" Castor cuts me off.

"Tell Max to call off his dogs. No, call off his father. Tell him to stop torturing your family who then turn around and torture my Lola for not marrying his stupid friend."

"Your Lola?" Luna clutches her chest and squints her eyes at me.

Smiling sheepishly, I tuck half my face behind Castor's bicep and nod.

Rolling her eyes, she scoffs. "Why would he listen to me? He wants to marry me. Unless I say yes, he's not going along with anything I ask."

"Just try. I've heard you can be very persuasive. I've never seen any evidence of it, but that's what I always heard." He rises and lowers his head to kiss me goodbye, leaving Luna stewing in her seat.

As I watch his tall figure walk away, I bite my lip and let out a soft squeal that annoys my sister.

"Isn't he the greatest thing since sliced bread?" I chuckle and feel my cheeks flush with heat.

Luna wrinkles her nose and scowls. "No! No, he's not."

FOURTEEN

CASTOR

Things are getting crazy, but I don't want to burden Lola with the details. It's not about keeping secrets. I love her, we're a team, but weddings are important to women and I don't want any extra stress on her right now. I don't care if we marry at City Hall, but she deserves her heart's desire and she's already been robbed of so much.

My girl hides her sorrow well. She's managed to plan a small wedding with the help of my mother, while bearing the heartache of her parents disowning her and preparing for a three-year move to France. I'll admit, I don't make things easy by demanding time for all my filthy urges.

She's such a trooper.

"Sweetheart, you can't mean nothing in three weeks." I protest Lola's insistence that we abstain until the wedding.

"Castor Kenneth Dewitt, we marry in sixteen days, that's not three weeks. Besides, next week is not a good time of the month for me, unless, of course, you wind up being as potent as you look." She laughs and I catch her arm, yanking her to me.

"Little girl, I'm going to show you just how potent I can be." Nudging her against a bar chair, I sit her down and push her skirt up.

She pushes it back down and makes a face.

"I know you think I'm your love slave, but I have some self-control, mister!"

Ignoring her, I fold it up slowly and seize her mouth like a beast, ravaging those luscious, pink lips and devour her alive. Her taste is the best aphrodisiac. The more I get, the more I want, and I always want everything.

"Castor!" Holding my finger over my mouth, I hush her, and her eyes grow wide with wonder. She won't stop me. She's too curious to stop me.

Bringing her ass forward, I peel off her panties, smelling them in front of her, inhaling her scent and delighting in the fact that I'll get to bask in the delicious aroma forever. My girl loves it when I'm nasty. It's been an absolute joy corrupting her and I'm nowhere near done. I've got so many plans--- the anticipation is killing me.

Spreading her legs, my hand seals tightly to her wet pussy and I part her seam, relishing the soft moans she can't contain. While we kiss, my fingers stroke her clit before digging deep into her moist channel.

"Castor! You're making this harder than it has to be." She squirms but grinds into my hand, whining whenever I pull it away. Since our first night together, I've taken pains to learn exactly what she needs and what drives her crazy. Every day, it becomes easier to reel her in.

I stroke gently, then harder, as her breath labors and her pout forms. Clawing at me, she nods her approval and I unzip. Holding my hard cock in my hand, I show it to her and make her ask for it.

"Is this what you want?"

She whimpers and nods enthusiastically, trying to reach for it.

"Well, why don't you come and get it?" I only want to tease her, but she doesn't have time for games.

Flying off the chair, she pushes me towards the sofa, straddles my hips and slides down my cock.

I gasp from the sting of her tight walls, clenching and squeezing me, but she doesn't flinch, she keeps going, bouncing on my dick, pulling off her shirt and then pushing her perfect tits in my face.

"Baby, I love you so much." I'm in awe of every move she makes. Chewing her lip, she arches her back and gyrates forward and back, riding me hard and shouting praise for my cock as she takes it all.

"I love you, Castor! Just this last time, ok?" Panting as she whines, she springs forward, shuddering in ecstasy as a climax twists through her small body.

I wind my fingers through her hair, pull her face to mine and kiss her wildly as our bodies grind and rut, shattering in a shared release that steals our breaths.

Wheezing, holding her tight, struggling for air, I shake my head.

"No, you can have five days, that's it."

She shakes her head but when I gaze at her and nod, she nods with me.

"Five? You...you promise?" Whimpering and shaking, she brings her lips to mine and waits for me to say the words.

"I promise. But I think you'll wish you hadn't made me." I wink and she hugs me, holding me close as she smothers my cheek with kisses.

"I'll stay home with Luna. Out of sight, out of mind."

I frown and grumble as I carry her to the shower. "You wouldn't be out of my mind if you were on the other side of the world, much less a few blocks away."

***

WHATEVER LUNA IS DOING, isn't working. Hugo Butler has recruited his wife, Jacinda, to pull money she'd previously promised to most of my family's friend's charities. Everyone is mad at us. Most have declined our wedding invitation for fear they'll upset the De Clare's and Butler's.

The Forsythe's are about to lose their family's ancestral home in Croton and will surely lose their home in the city before the end of the year. And most concerning, if Lola isn't pregnant, my parents want me to call this off.

They can both kiss my ass and kiss it hard.

Lola is not negotiable. I'm not leaving for Paris without her and she will go as my wife. She doesn't know the full extent, yet. Luna has asked me not to tell her until she can speak to Max, again. I don't blame her. Not really. I want to, but that's not fair. No one wants to be bullied into being with someone and although I suspect she likes Max more than she'll admit, I'm not sure what he believes he'll accomplish with this strategy.

I asked around and everyone who knows him swears he's not a bad guy. He's just madly in love with Luna and won't give up until they're together.

Poor guy. All that work and in the end, he'll wind up with Luna Forsythe.

FIFTEEN

LOLA

"Lola, do you have a tampon?" Luna barges into my room while I busy myself, packing.

"No, sorry. But you're not due yet, why do you need one?" I stare at her. She's nervous and fidgeting.

"I'm seeing Max. I'd like to discourage him from putting the moves on me later in the evening. I thought I could let a tampon accidentally fall out of my purse over dinner. My friend, Geneva gave me the idea."

"That is so dumb." I roll my eyes and frown.

"I know, but so is Geneva. And anything helps. Max... is... well, he can be very persuasive."

Something's up. Luna has no trouble turning men down. She could put that skill on her resume. Yet, somehow, Max Butler, the man she claims to hate most, is her kryptonite.

"Luna?"

"Yeah?"

"Are you in love with him?" I walk into my closet, leaving her to contemplate her answer before she lies.

"No! You know I'm not." She huffs and tries to hide the panic in her voice.

"I only know that you say you're not. And I've never really thought to ask before. Why is he so special? Why can't you say no?" I bring out more clothes and she shakes her head, as if she's trying to shake thoughts from forming in her mind.

"I have said no. He asked me to marry him and I said no. I just like the sex. He's better than... no, he's the best. I don't really hate him. I just hate that I feel so weak around him." Burying her face in her hands, she pulls her hair and screams.

"Lola! What am I going to do? I lose this place next month. Mom and Dad aren't paying for anything anymore. I've tried to find a better job, but everyone keeps telling me they're not hiring. I think I'm blackballed. You're leaving. And there's a gorgeous billionaire with a magic cock begging to marry me, promising he'll solve all my problems. But I don't think I can do it." For the first time in years, I watch my sister cry and my heart breaks for her.

And this isn't a little sniffle at the end of a sad movie. This is ugly blubbering with snot, tissues and gasps for air.

"Luna! Dammit woman, are you in love with him?!"

She shakes her head, then stops and gazes at me. She's scared. "I don't know. I don't think so."

I don't believe her, but she's crying, and I won't make things worse by arguing.

"Then don't marry him. I love you. You can come live with Castor and I in Paris until you get off your feet. Just let me run it by him, okay?" I hug her tight and she cries harder.

"Lola! I can't stand Castor. And he would kill me for accepting and ruining your honeymoon period." She pulls away and wipes her tears.

"I know what I have to do." Steeling her resolve, she ducks her head and nods. "I know how to make everything right."

"Luna, you better not agree to marry him!" Chasing after her, I catch her just before she locks herself in her bedroom.

"Just trust your sister. I know what to do." She closes her door, but as I walk away, she swings it open again.

"Why don't you have tampons? You should have started days ago?"

I shrug my shoulders. "I'm out. I need to get more."

No, I'm just late.

SIXTEEN

CASTOR

"Just like that? You threaten to disinherit me, disown me, not show up to my wedding and you have the balls to tell me everything is forgiven? By whom? Not by me!" I bellow a litany of insults on both my parents and they sit there and take it all.

"Darling, we'd never do such a thing. This whole fiasco has been incredibly stressful. You marry in five days and people are sending last minute RSVPs." My mother leads me to the couch and shows me the stack of replies.

I stand, adjust my cuffs, tug my jacket and straighten my tie. They will be pissed. "Lola and I married this morning at City Hall. We won't be attending this affair." I take an invitation and toss it to the floor.

Both shoot up and scream at the same time. "Castor! How could you?"

"As soon as Luna agreed to marry Max, everything went back to normal, or at least everyone wants to pretend none of this happened.

Lola was disowned and because her sister took a bullet for the family, she's tormented by guilt for being a part of that. We don't want her parents attending and it will look strange if we have a big wedding without them." I attempt to exit but they rush to stop me.

"Castor! Everything is paid. You should at least have a reception with dancing and cake." My mother blocks the door.

"We're doing that when I get home. I ordered a cake, and I've picked out a nice song for dancing. *John Lennon*. It'll be perfect. We don't need all the pomp and guests to feel married. Plus, Lola might already be expecting. We'll know soon."

"A baby? So soon! Kenneth, do something!" My mother begs me to reconsider while she badgers my father to order me to attend this reception. She can't help it. It's who she is.

"Let me speak to my wife. I'll call you in the morning." I storm out, pretending to be furious. I just want to get home to Lola.

As soon as we decided to marry on the sly four days ago, she cut me off. I put up a good argument, but she made a valid and logical point. We scheduled the abstinence period to commence five days before our wedding, not the wedding date.

That little weasel.

Racing into our building, I tug off my tie as I fly into the elevator. With my neighbors watching me on our ride up, I remove my cuff links and toss them in my pocket.

"It's my wedding night." I smile and nod.

Their discomfort immediately ends. Smiling with relief, they congratulate me as I run off and skid down the hall towards our door.

"Lola!" I throw my jacket on the floor and undo my belt.

"Lola! Baby! Where are you?"

"Well, hello, Mr. Dewitt." My heart stops. No, it's my eyes. For a moment, I don't think I'm seeing right, but when she walks towards me, so much blood rushes to my cock, I think I might faint.

"Sweetheart? Is that your white bikini? The one from..." My mouth slacks and words leave me.

"The very one." Sashaying across our living room in her bare feet, she draws near and begins unbuttoning my shirt. "How about you show me all the things you thought about doing to me in this white bikini? How does that sound, baby?"

She walks away, curling her finger for me to follow her before heading into our bedroom. I'm so stunned, I watch her ass shake and feel come drip out of my cock, before I finally snap out of my daze.

Hauling ass into the bedroom, I flip her over and toss her into the bed.

"Castor!" She squeals and giggles as I tear off my shirt, kick off my shoes and pull off my pants.

"Baby, there are so many fantasies. I'm going to keep you up all night." Ripping off her bottoms, I remember the tattoo. Where's the tattoo? I never thought to look or ask about it before now.

"Didn't you have a tat? I could have sworn I saw one in those photos." I examine her closer, checking if she had it removed.

"It was a fake."

She thinks for a moment. "Wow, baby. You really were a stalker. I made sure it wasn't visible in case my parents saw those photos."

Spreading her long thighs, I grin as I slink my face towards her gushing pussy. "Guilty as charged. You found me out, Lola. Too bad you married a horrible, unrepentant stalker before you learned the truth."

Inhaling deeply, I shudder as her scent fills my nostrils, making my mouth water and slack at the same time. With one hand caressing her abdomen, I take her by the waist and bring her forward.

"I love you, Lola. Thank you for marrying me." In less than five weeks, I got everything I wanted. I have her and we have a baby on the way. I didn't want to give my parents the details because for now, this baby is ours. Just like she's mine and I'm hers.

"I love you, Castor." She holds my hand over her non-existent belly. "Thank you for asking me and for this." We kiss and as always, the entire world disappears except for us. She's so beautiful and smart and sweet and sexy and kind. I know I don't deserve her.

But she's mine.

SEVENTEEN

LOLA

I had to tell Luna. He can't expect me to keep my sister in the dark after everything she did for the family. Besides, she guessed it for herself. One damn comment that my boobs hurt, and she was onto me in seconds.

We're not counting today as our official wedding date. That was four days ago. It might have been small and fast with only Max and Luna as our witnesses, but that was more than enough. As long as Castor was the one standing next to me, I don't care where the hell we married.

But it's nice to make some use out of this dress. I feel like such a princess.

The hypocrisy of wearing white after Castor sexed me up all night and while I'm five weeks pregnant, isn't lost on me, but who cares? I have my man. I have his baby and we're moving to Paris next week.

Oh, I'm going to miss my sister!

"Come dance with me, Mrs. Dewitt." Castor takes my hand and leads me to the floor. We've been dancing all night. It's his way of avoiding small talk and his mother's constant questions about the existence of a possible grandchild.

"Have I told you, you look stunning?" He leans in and whispers in my ear.

"No, sir. You've called me beautiful, gorgeous, magnificent, and incredible but there has been no mention of stunning."

"I'm despicable." He croons in my ear and the sound of his deep voice fills me with visions of all the lovely things ahead. I'm so in love with him. I didn't think he'd be so perfect. Reality always falls short of your fantasies, but Castor is so much better. He's the fantasy I never dared to consider.

"Sweetheart, are you okay?" He hands me his hanky to wipe my tears. I've always worn my heart on my sleeve, but these pregnancy hormones are really cramping my style. I cry with everything now.

"I'm just happy. I have you. I have everything."

"No, I do." He kisses my nose.

"No, I do." I tease.

"No, you know I do." He laughs but halts at the sound of Luna's voice.

"Cut that out, please." She pushes him aside and gives me a big bear hug.

"We're leaving. I won't see you until you come back because this heartless man is kidnapping you to a foreign country." She sniffles against my shoulder.

"I'll be back before your wedding. It's only three months away." I hug her tighter and watch Castor and Max stare at one another awkwardly, waiting for us to finish the sister cry-fest.

"You better take care of her!" She hits Castor in the chest and storms off, leaving Max to apologize and slink away.

Jumping into my husband's arms, I kiss his chest and gaze up into those gray-blue eyes. "It's getting late, baby and we have a plane to catch in the morning."

"This is a second wedding night, Lola. You're not sleeping. Rules are rules. You're busting out that bikini for round two."

EIGHTEEN

EPILOGUE- 3 MONTHS LATER

CASTOR

We're having a girl. At first, Lola was adamant about waiting until the birth to learn the sex, but thirty seconds after we walked out, she ran back in and insisted they tell her. We both had a feeling she was a girl and confirming it just helps us plan everything.

That's the line she keeps repeating and I've been instructed to follow her lead.

Paris has been an adventure. We'd both been here before, but coming together, moving here and setting up our first real home for our family feels out of this world. While we can, before the baby comes, we explore every chance we get. Work takes me around the country and into a few neighboring nations, but while she's able, my Lola comes with me. It will break my heart when she can't.

But that will only be temporary. Our family will go places together.

Next week we head out for Luna and Max's wedding. I'm still not sure about those two. He's a lot nicer than I expected, which makes me pity him even more for loving Luna so much. And goddamn, does he love Luna. I think he loves her the way I love Lola, but she's not Lola. Anyway, it's not my business, but I think there's something missing. With her, not him.

But it will be good for Lola to see her sister again.

I just hope she goes through with it.

NINETEEN

EPILOGUE- 8 YEARS LATER

"Hold it right there. Where are you going?"

Castor calls out to me from his office, while I ready the kids to go swimming.

"I need to get your son into his trunks. Maddie and Betsy have gone outside to greet your mother and if I don't get these shorts on Callum, she will leave him here."

"Cal! Get your behind in here, young man. Your grandmother is waiting for you." Rushing over to retrieve his naked, petulant son, Castor turns him upside down, slips his swim trunks on and delivers him to Viola on the deck.

"Make sure she brings them back in time for dinner!" I holler from the bedroom while I make a quick change.

When he returns, Castor cracks a wide smile. "Baby, where did that come from?"

Wearing a tiny, stars and stripes bikini, I strut towards my gorgeous husband and slip my hand into the top of his pants.

"We're in the Hamptons, it's Fourth of July, this is where I first fell in love with you," I bring my lips to his and he lunges to me, surprising me with the intensity of his kiss. Lifting me off the ground, he carries me to bed and falls in with me.

"And you were wearing a much tamer version of a stars and stripes bathing suit. You, naughty girl. I believe your old one was a one-piece." He unknots my top and cups my breasts, making me shiver with desire.

"I'm Castor's naughty girl, aren't I?"

His grins and dips his head, taking a hard nipple into his warm mouth. Suckling hard, he pulls and teases my flesh, driving me to the brink. Holding him closer, I pull the shirt over his head, run my hands down his muscular back and will him to take me and take me hard.

"You're my angel but you're also one hell of naughty girl, baby." He chuckles as he pushes me up the mattress, unties my bottoms and sinks his face in my pussy. Spreading my thighs wider for him, I watch him lick and feather my clit, driving me wild with every stroke of his tongue. Overcome by his talents, I pant and thrash, trembling in his grasp as he sends me into another world.

"Baby, I want you. Please, give it to me." He knows what that means and he's ready. Pulling his pants down, he edges closer to my face and feeds me his hard cock. I can't take it all, but I can take most of it and he loves watching me do it. As it slides down my throat, I pump his shaft, stroking, swallowing, and begging for him to come on me.

"Not today."

"Please, Castor." I whine, childishly.

"No, sweetheart. Come here." Taking me into his arms, he crushes his lips to mine, covers me with his body and pushes his cock in slowly. Gazing into my eyes, he never breaks contact. While he thrusts and plunges deep, caressing my body, moaning and groaning with every stroke, his gray-blue eyes never leave me. Locked in this trance, I grind into him, arching my back while my hips rise to meet his over and over again. It's never enough. I'll never get enough of him.

"I love you." He whispers, as he brings me into his arms and erupts with a low growl, overcome with emotion.

"I love you." I kiss his sweaty chest and relax into his arms.

"No, I love you, more." He laughs.

"No, I love you, more."

"No, me."

"Where's my lemonade, sir?"

"Coming right up, little lady." He runs into the kitchen, sweaty and naked.

Life is wonderful.

THERE SHE GOES

THERE
She Goes

A SUMMER BRIDE DUET, BOOK 2
MATILDA MARTEL

ONE

LUNA

I don't tell people about the way Max and I met. Everyone assumes it was a horrible date that went so badly, I cut him out of my life, ghosting him for months on end. But it wasn't. It was one of the sweetest dates I'd ever had, and although he wanted to take it slower, I came on to him, inviting him in, trying to make it into something casual.

It backfired.

As he has done time and time again, Max not only surprised me, he changed me. Every time we're together, he does not leave me as he found me. And it makes me crazy.

I don't know how he does it, but it's infuriating.

I know that doesn't make sense to most people. Love is rare. *I know that!* Not everyone gets to fall in love and if you are lucky enough to feel the kind of love I feel for this ridiculous man, I would tell you--- no, I would insist that you hold on to him and never let go. But you're not me and I don't have a normal heart.

I don't want to love anyone this much. Not now. Not ever.

But it's a lovely story. There are nights when I'm alone in my room, thinking about every little detail of that glorious day and I'm moved to tears recalling his smile, the way the light shone in his pale green eyes when he leaned in to kiss me, the flex of his muscular arms when he rowed the small boat that took us out into the lake and the feel of his hand in mine when we walked into town to grab a bite to eat.

It felt like something out of a movie. How the hell does anyone else compete with that?

Well, no one else has. I haven't been with anyone since he and I first got together two years ago, which makes it easy for him to break my resolve and worm his way back into my life every few months.

Why does he keep trying?

I'm horrible to him. I say terrible, hurtful things that should send him running for the hills, but he doesn't give up. He says he needs me. He needs *us*. He insists I need him too, and he's fighting for our future. That's so pathetic.

No, it's beautiful. I know, it is. I have a heart... it just doesn't work the same.

My family has a hotel business, we've had it for generations, and the oldest hotel is in Croton, an hour north of the city. It's a gorgeous little town. After I finished college, I spent a few weeks up there, living out of my grandparent's old house and helping at the hotel every other day. It was a mini-vacation. A small present *from Luna to Luna, with love.*

It was late May, just before Memorial Day weekend and the air was still fresh before the unbearable heat of summer. Donning one of the cutest sundresses I've ever owned, pink, not my typical color, but it was Croton and no one important would see me, I ventured out into town to grab a cup of coffee and some pastries for the hotel staff.

It was such a pretty day. The sun was shining, the streets were virtually deserted, and as I reached for the door to The Black Dog Coffee Shop, a tall, dark-haired man with stunning, green eyes jumped in front and opened it for me.

It was a chivalrous act. He didn't linger or ask my name. Holding his gaze as I stood there, so unaccustomed to nice gestures, I was uncertain if he was trying to be a gentleman or just attempting to beat me inside. Smiling oddly, he finally nodded and waved me through. Although, I hustled in and behaved unaffected--- I felt weak. There was something about him. Something that clicked. It was as if my heart had been sleeping for twenty-two years and with one smile, in one second, it woke up and started beating.

At first, we didn't speak. I nervously perused the pastry display case and signaled for him to pass me in line. The clerk already knew his order, but he made small talk and spoke politely with everyone behind the counter. That might seem like nothing to note, but this is New York and he and I live in Manhattan. Some-times, the people who grow up with the most privilege, the ones who should know better, are the worst offenders. Max isn't like that. He has a soul.

Standing next to him, my interest only grew stronger. Listening to the sound of his voice, the inflection, the warmth behind the depth and inhaling the intoxicating scent of his cologne made me lose my train of thought. By the time I was done, I'd purchased two dozen different muffins and tarts to take back to the hotel and I wasn't sure I'd be able to carry them all on my own. Max gallantly offered his services.

On our walk back, we talked about Columbia. He graduated law school a year earlier, and I'd just finished a journalism degree. We discovered we only lived a few blocks from one another in the city and had several friends in common. He made me laugh. I teased, and he gave it back, which I appreciated. Eventually, we made plans to go for a boat ride, which turned into a picnic and a stroll into town for dinner later that evening. It was the most romantic day I'd ever experienced fully clothed.

I never make things so easy for men, but there was something gnawing inside me, wanting to spend time with him, wanting to listen to his voice a little longer and gaze into those green eyes for as long as I could. I should have stopped it, but I couldn't. Seriously. Love was unfamiliar to me. I mistook it for lust, a crazy, school girl lust that would surely disappear once we had sex.

It didn't. That night changed my life.

TWO

MAX

I've never wanted anything in this world more than I want Luna Forsythe. From the moment I laid eyes on her, I never stood a chance. She sunk her hooks in me without ever trying. That's her secret. She doesn't try. She doesn't need to. One glimpse at those adorable curves, that auburn hair, those icy blue eyes and I was ruined. But she's more than just a beautiful girl. She's smart and funny, she doesn't put up with anyone's shit and despite what anyone thinks, she has a heart.

She has a big heart.

Luna wants everyone to believe nothing gets to her. No one breaks through. No one touches her. But I know better. I've seen the person she keeps hidden. It's been my privilege knowing the woman she really is under that icy front and that's the girl I love. *That's my Luna.* No one gets to see that side of her, but me.

Well, maybe her sister.

My friends think I'm crazy. No one understands why I hold on. But none of them have ever been in love and they don't understand this kind of love comes around once in a lifetime, and only if we're lucky enough to find it. Finding Luna was easy. Making her fall in love with me was easy. Getting her to admit it, has been nearly impossible.

But I'm not giving up. I can't.

Sadly, this has been going on much longer for me than it has for her. She thinks it started in Croton, but I lost my heart to Luna years before we ever met. I knew who she was, everyone knows all about Luna Forsythe. There isn't a guy living in the Upper East Side and probably Upper West who hasn't tried to make a pass at my girl. She's fucking gorgeous, the epitome of sex, like a young Rita Hayworth. It's maddening. But she makes you put in so much work, most give up before they ever get to first base. And she prefers it that way.

Luna can't be bothered with most people.

Every time I saw her, my heart ached to inch closer, touch her, speak to her, say something that might make a difference, but I feared ruining things. Although we lived a few blocks away from one another, we didn't run in the same circles. Luna's family is on the New York Social Registry. They're old money. And old money doesn't like my kind.

These families are all the same. My father worked for everything he has, and has ten times more than they do, but as far as they're concerned, his money is too new. He's trash, which makes me trash. They love us when it comes time to fund their charities or invest in their failing business ventures, but most of the times we're excluded from their events because we're *nouveau riche.* I didn't approach Luna because I didn't want to find out she was as snobby as I imagined. I didn't want to ruin the fantasy with a harsh reality. In my mind, she was perfect.

But I was wrong. She wasn't like them. I took my chance because I couldn't bear another second being apart. I knew once we came together, once we were truly one, things would work out between us. I know Luna and I are meant to be together. Nothing can convince me otherwise.

Our day in Croton felt like magic. I knew she was there. I'd planned our meeting for weeks ahead of time. When I arrived, I ventured to that coffee shop every day hoping to get there at just the right time. After five days, it finally worked.

Gazing into her eyes for the first time, I felt her recognize me. She knew I was there for her and slowly but surely, she let down one wall after the next. By the time I took her home, she was fighting to bring them back up. I wouldn't let her. She wanted to keep things casual. She thought I'd let her get away with turning what was happening between us into something cheap and insignificant.

But I didn't.

I think about that night often. Perhaps, I pushed too hard or expected too much too soon but making love to her changed me.

It was pouring when I took her home. We raced from the car to her grandparent's porch, underneath my windbreaker, laughing the whole way when we both almost slipped. The last thing I wanted to do was leave. The thought was torture, but there wasn't any rush to take things further. We'd both be in Croton for another week and have so much time to ourselves. Luna had other plans.

"Please, don't go. Storms frighten me. It's silly and I hate appearing like a damsel in distress, but I sent everyone home earlier this week." She wrapped her arms around my waist and pressed her cheek to my chest. How could I say no?

Reaching down to lift her chin, I lowered my head and grazed her lips gently. Tasting her, I focused on the color of her eyes and made this memory, never wanting to forget any little part of that night.

"Do you really want me to stay?"

Chewing her bottom lip, she ducked her head and whispered, "Yes."

"Storm or no storm, I'm coming back tomorrow, Luna. This isn't a one-time thing."

Her eyes flew open. No one spoke to her that way. She gave the commands. She never received them. But before she could protest, I seized her mouth, and showered her with one fiery kiss after another. Seconds later, her weak challenge died with a moan, as she melted in my embrace.

Curling her arms around my neck, she let me lift her off the ground and whimpered something inaudible into my mouth.

"What?"

"Up the stairs, first door on the left. My bedroom." She purred, sweetly, seeking my lips out for another kiss as I sprinted up the stairs.

Greedy with lust and eager to please the woman I loved, I took two steps at a time, kicked open the door and set her carefully on the bed. We gazed at one another, waiting to see who would make the first move, who would reach for a zipper or button and it was Luna. Fluttering her eyelashes nervously, she undid her sash and tugged the dress off her shoulders.

It was something out of a dream.

My pulse raced. She was my heart's desire, the object of each one of my fantasies for over two years and she was offering herself to me. Before she could pull it all the way off, I kicked off my shoes, pulled down my pants and tugged away my shirt. But my eyes never left hers.

Giggling with surprise, she covered her mouth and waved me on the bed, taking my hand in hers. She tried to take the lead and as much as I wanted to see where she would take us, I knew where we were going. I refused to be someone to get out of her system. We were making love. I was staying the night and Luna Forsythe would be mine.

Straddling my hips, smiling with a naughty deviance, she made her move. It was a risk, but I shook my head and turned us over, pulling her hands over her head. She looked pissed, but before she could anger, I reclaimed her lips and deepened our kiss. She moaned then shuddered as I swallowed her complaints, with one kiss after another, devouring those perfect lips. As our tongues danced, and her tense body surrendered in my arms, I brought my hands down to her breasts and molded them to her smooth, supple flesh, before releasing each one from their lacy confinement.

Feeling her warm, heavy breasts in my hands, her taut nipples between my fingers drove my desire over the edge. I wanted a closer peek, to feel them in my mouth, on my tongue, inhaling their scent and imagine I was the last man who would ever touch them again. Searing a path from her mouth, down her neck and chest, I took her hard flesh in my mouth, licking and suckling, engulfing as much as I could until I heard her moans grow louder and her pleas grow stronger.

I wanted to end my torment and sate my hunger, but there was another taste I needed first.

Dipping my head lower, my teeth raked her hot skin as I traveled down her stomach, kneading and nibbling on her flesh. The closer I drew, the more the scent of her arousal filled my senses and I couldn't deny myself what I knew in my heart was mine, what was always meant to be mine and always would be after that night.

Writhing in my grasp, Luna whimpered my name, asking me to stop, then silently mouthed the words, "don't stop", as she raised her hips salaciously, wanting more, but terrified to say how much she needed it, how much she needed me.

"Let go, Luna. Let go." Spreading her thighs, I slowly lowered my mouth into her moist pussy, licking her folds, tracing her slit, then greedily buried my tongue in her sleek channel.

"Max! Please." Her cries of ecstasy felt louder than the thunder clapping over the house.

Drowning in her taste, I feasted without mercy, stabbing my tongue deep, watching her tremble in a fit of desire, moaning and writhing as she called my name. I couldn't take enough, and she only wanted to give me more.

Lifting her hips, I fed ravenously, listening to her screams, feeling her twists, waiting for the perfect moment to focus on her sweet spot and bring her to the release she so desperately craved. While I stroked her clit with my tongue, I fingered her deep, held her down with my shoulders as her hips pumped, her legs thrashed, and her torso trembled through the sounds of incoherent squeals and gasps. First, she begged me to go faster, then she pleaded with me to slow down. I ignored her voice and listened to her body. Her shuddering limbs gave everything away.

"Come for me, Luna. Let go, baby."

Gasping for air and overcome with a savage surge of adrenaline, she arched her back and howled as her hips rocked wildly against my face taking the rest of her body into a fit of ecstasy that only ceased when I rose between her thighs and slid my cock into her quivering pussy.

"Max, oh God, Max." She whispered, wrapping her legs around my waist, pulling me closer and covering my mouth with hers.

Holding my hand, she looked into my eyes as my shaft stretched her open, widening my path and slowly rocking her into a state of bliss.

She was soaked, but so tight, I struggled to fill her. Lifting her hips to improve my angle, I drove harder, deeper, until she pushed down and helped me bury my length inside her.

"Baby, you're so tight. Am I hurting you?"

She shook her head. "No, please keep going."

"I won't, Luna. I won't stop. Not until you come all over my cock."

Her mouth shot open in feigned offense seconds before her lips curved into a lusty grin. I tried to slow my pace, wanting to last as long as I could, but the torment was unbearable. Pulling out, I thrust back in harder, bringing her lips back to mine as she nodded her approval.

"Give it to me, Max. I need it. You feel so fucking good."

She whispered in my ear, as I brought her tighter into my arms, repeating the motion until the friction of my cock forcing its way in, pushing her walls open, stretching her to the limit, sent us both into a trance of primal lust. With every stroke, I drove deeper, savoring a more intense pleasure than I'd ever experienced. When her wails grew stronger, I felt her freeze, gasping in fear as she held on to the edge of the cliff, refusing to let go.

She wasn't going to do that to us.

"Let go, Luna. Don't fight this. Let go, baby."

She fought harder, turning her face even as her body continued to demand more, meeting each thrust until she shook with a growing tension in search of deliverance. When I captured her mouth in a blistering kiss, thrusting, groaning and growling, taking everything that belonged to me, giving her everything that was hers, she couldn't hold on. She tried, but I gave her no choice.

She was coming whether she liked it or not.

Cupping her ass, I brought her hips off the bed and I drove all the way in.

"Max! Oh, no!"

"Let go, Luna!"

Screams of ecstasy escaped her lips as she shattered in my arms. As she wailed and writhed in a fit of pleasure, I dropped her and stroked her clit into a third and fourth orgasm, licking her nipples, plunging without mercy until her clenching pussy squeezed the come out of my cock, sending me falling forward into her shivering limbs.

I lost count how many times we made love that night and every single time, I had to coax her to let go.

In the morning, I told her I loved her.

An hour later she drove back to New York and refused to see me or speak to me for three months.

That's Luna.

THREE

LUNA

"Luna, this is your fault. We need to speak with your sister. Where is she?" Our parents barge into our apartment and the only reason I let them in is because I fear resources are about to be pulled. They look furious and ready for a fight.

"Lola is with Castor and the Dewitt's. They're shooting engagement photos in the park. How the hell is this my fault? Lola just saved you ten million dollars and more time to pay Ken Dewitt. How is this a bad thing?" I walk into the kitchen and try to ignore the two voices competing in volume to chastise me like I just came home drunk from a party.

"Engagement photos? So soon! This will look terrible!" My mother covers her mouth and falls into the couch.

"Lola is marrying Castor. You're not changing her mind. You wanted me to marry him. Why are you acting like this is such a terrible thing?" I pour myself some water and reach for my phone. As discreet as possible, I text a warning to Lola, who is on her way home.

"We had our own solution. You've both cost us an incredible amount of money and the wrath of both the De Clare's and the Butler's." Daddy points his finger at me, before heading to the fridge to look for something to snack on.

"The Butler's? What the hell do the Butler's have to do with this?" I demand an answer, switching my glare between both, unsure who is behind dragging Max into this.

When neither confess, I pounce on my mother. "You! You said you wanted me to marry Max, not Castor. Why? Why are they involved? Since when are you a friend of Hugo Butler? You don't know him. Someone better confess, or I'm calling Max and ruining whatever schemes you have planned." I stomp my fists on the counter.

Two years ago, when they heard I was seen all over Croton and a few times in Manhattan with Maxwell Butler, the only son of a man who could buy and sell my parents and most of their friends several times over, they treated me like I'd just scandalized the family name. Their derision is one reason I let him back in my life. I didn't want him or anyone else believing I walked away for such an asinine reason.

Max was wonderful. It was me. It was always me. He deserved better.

"Lola was supposed to marry Orson De Clare, not Castor Dewitt. Theo De Clare plans to buy the hotel in Croton, renovate it, and gift it to Orson and Lola as a wedding present. It would have stayed in our family and given me the money to keep our hotel in the city from being snatched up by creditors. But you ruined it by encouraging her to accept that philanderer's proposal!" He raises his voice to make his point.

"Me? No. Lola loves Castor. Lola's always loved Castor. There is no way in hell you're talking her out of marrying him. Yesterday, she devoted an entire hour to ordering her new stationary with her new name. This is her dream come true."

"Elmer! Enough about Lola. Luna can still marry Max." My mother rushes over, arms flailing in panic.

"Luna, Hugo Butler has offered to invest heavily in our hotels in Manhattan, Newport and Greenwich, giving his share to Max when you marry. He says Maxwell is in love with you. He says you and he have carried on for the last few years in secret. If you have feelings for him, why won't you consider him?!" She reaches out for me, but I back away, furious that she would invade my privacy with her gossip.

I can't believe I'm hearing the words Max, love and marriage come out of my mother's mouth. This is a nightmare.

"Hugo Butler doesn't know what he's talking about. I told you I don't like Max. I can't stand him. I'm not marrying him! Your best bet is to kiss Ken Dewitt's ass and hope he or Castor lend you more money." I stammer in my anger, too upset to look either in the eye. Just before I run out of the room, Lola arrives and they both descend on her.

"What are you doing here? Luna! What's the matter?" Lola drops her things and tries to follow me, but she's surrounded.

By the time I reach my bedroom, I can't prevent the tears welling in my eyes from streaming down my cheeks. Rushing to the bathroom, I wash my face with cold water and try to talk myself out of this grief. No one can see me this way. They'll think I have feelings for him. It's no one's business how I feel. I'm not marrying him. Just because I love him. Do I? Do I love him? It makes no difference. Even if I do, we're not right for each other.

I'm not right for anyone.

FOUR

MAX

"Well, you were right, Luna rejected Castor." Orson scowls as he shakes off his raincoat and hangs it behind his chair. She may not want to marry me, but I know Luna enough to bet money she wouldn't allow her parents to select her husband, especially someone like Castor.

I don't know him personally, but I heard he gets around.

"Why do you look so upset?" I call the waitress over. I'm desperate for a drink. For the past two hours, ever since I found out it was storming tonight, I've been fighting a hard-on and texting Luna. She always replies during storms. She can't help herself.

He clenches his fists and shakes them in the air. "I'm not upset. I'm fucking enraged. That son of a bitch is marrying my Lola, instead!"

I stare at him in disbelief. I should have expected something like this, but I've been too wrapped up in Luna to give his plans very much thought outside of how they could help me. She's mentioned her sister's longtime crush on Castor. We've laughed about how long she's carried a torch for him, hardly dating anyone else in hopes of one day realizing her dream of becoming Mrs. Castor Dewitt.

"So, he just switched girls? They were interchangeable for him?" I'm glad he doesn't want Luna, but I feel bad for Lola. She deserves better than someone like that.

When the waitress hands him a glass of whiskey, he downs it in one gulp before asking for another.

"No! This is what he wanted all along. He can't stand Luna. The only reason he agreed to the arrangement was because he and Luna called a truce and staged a scene at her parent's house. Luna threw a tantrum, offered Lola in exchange and Castor jumped at his chance. Lola is already wearing a fucking engagement ring!" He's so mad, his face has turns bright red as he shouts.

"We had a date scheduled later this week, and she sent me a message to cancel. It was a sweet message. She apologized and wished me well. Then I found out they took engagement photos yesterday morning in Central Park and it's being announced in the *New York* fucking *Times* this weekend! How the fuck does that horny little bastard just come out of nowhere and steal my Lola!"

I want to find out more for him. If Luna was in on it, she must have determined he was sincere in his feelings. No matter how badly her sister wanted Castor, she wouldn't lift a finger to help him if she believed he had ill intentions. She adores Lola.

After waiting the appropriate time to listen to Orson's rant and dishing out the required sympathy, I lie and say I have to meet my father. I'm not sure how to feel about his desire to be with Lola if she genuinely wants to be with Castor and he wants to be with her.

Racing through the rain, I check my messages and see Luna has started a text that was never completed. That girl will be the death of me. It's been two months since I've seen her, and I don't know how much longer I can take. Five steps away from entering my building, I keep walking. I've had enough. She can't keep doing this to us. I know she's mad at me for pushing her about getting married. It's dumb when she won't even acknowledge she loves me. But what else can I do? I've loved her for so long and I know she loves me. I feel stupid for saying it when she keeps pushing me away. But I know she does.

That's why it's so hard to let go. None of this makes any sense.

Storming through her building, I pass by the doorman with ease. She doesn't know I own her place. It makes it easier to keep an eye on her this way. Yesterday, her parents pulled her lease. She'll need to move in two months and I'm not so sure they'll welcome her back home. They have plans and they don't intend on making things easy for her.

The last thing I want to do is help them push her into a corner, but she won't talk to me. She won't tell me why she's so afraid of being together. Last year, when we were at our happiest, she promised she'd see a shrink and I'm not sure if she ever did because she cut me off for months after we discussed it.

When I reach her floor, the sound of rolling thunder echoes through the hall and I hear a text come in seconds before I reach for the doorbell.

Luna: *Max? Are you nearby?*

Me: *Come, let me in. I'm here, baby.*

She opens the door and her beautiful, tear-stained face appears through the crack. It's not the storm. Something else is upsetting her.

I push through and take her limp body into my arms. Helping her wrap her long legs around my waist, I walk us to the living room as she rests her heavy head on my shoulder.

"What's wrong, sweetheart? Why are you crying?" I whisper as I rock her gently.

Her breath hitches. "Max, I missed you." She buries her head in my neck and exhales deeply.

"But that's not why you're crying?"

She shakes her head and sighs with sadness as I set her on the couch.

"Lola's getting married. She's so happy and I'm happy for her, but Castor's taking her to France in five weeks. She's my little sister. Who will take care of her?"

Removing my jacket, I crawl in next to her and as usual, she rests her head on my lap.

"I guess, Castor will. That's what husbands do." Stroking her hair, I let myself settle into her world. This happens every few weeks or months. Luna lets me back in and my heart is finally at peace again. I can't keep doing this. After she gets her fix, she sends me away and I wait. Every night, I wait. Like an idiot, I wait for something as simple as this.

I should leave. I should leave her hanging for once. I hate playing games, but she should know what it feels like. Just once.

"Why are you helping the De Clare's?" She gazes up at me, her blue eyes wide with curiosity.

"You know I don't give a damn about Orson. This is about you, Luna. His father introduced my father to yours. He's broke and we can help your family."

She sits up and glares at me. "Why do you want to marry me, Max? You know how I feel about getting married. I'll be a terrible wife."

"No, you wouldn't. You're good at everything you do, everything that matters to you. Why don't I matter?" I run my hand through my hair in exasperation, trying to control my anger.

"It wasn't my idea to use these circumstances to talk you into marrying me, but I don't know what else to do with you. Why do you keep doing this to us?"

Speechless and sad, she gazes at me with remorse before bowing her head in defeat.

"I'm sorry." She whispers.

I believe her. I know she's sorry. And so am I.

"I'm sorry you feel sad, sweetheart, but I better go." Reaching for my jacket, I stand and head towards the door. It isn't as difficult as I imagined. My heart is breaking but I've grown accustomed to it.

I've learned to walk it off.

FIVE

LUNA

I'm broken. Something inside me broke long ago and I don't know how to fix it. I don't talk about it with anyone, not even Lola because that's not the person I want to be. *Broken Luna* is not the person I want the world to see.

But no one sees that person more than Max.

I've spent my life terrified of falling in love, paralyzed with fear that someone will wield that kind of power over me. It's not normal. I know it's not. But I can't remember how it feels to be normal anymore.

Except once in a while, when I'm in his arms and the world disappears, I'm not afraid. For those few hours or days, I think I'll be okay. I make myself believe he and I will be happy, finally happy and in love, the way I know, in my heart, we're meant to be. But then I run or worse, I push him away.

I don't want to push him away anymore. I miss him every single day he's not with me.

"Max."

His back is to me and my voice is so soft, I fear he hasn't heard me. Halfway out the door, he stops.

"Did you say something?" His voice is raspy and faint.

"Yes. Please don't go." I choke on every word.

"Why?" He turns to face me, and his eyes are red with tears.

"Because I don't want you to leave. Please." I blink heavy tears as I agonize over every word.

After locking the door, he returns.

"That's not good enough. Tell me what I want to hear, and I'll stay."

I gaze up at him, afraid to speak and still unwilling to speak the words I've mumbled to myself, behind his back for two years.

He steps closer and wipes an errant tear. "Say it, Luna. I don't for one second believe you don't mean it."

"Say it. Tell me you love me, and I promise, I'll always fight for us."

"Max..."

Gazing into the soft green eyes that first captured my heart, I summon the courage to tell him what I should have said that very first night we were together. I felt it then, but I've spent the last two years denying it to him and myself.

"I love you. I've always loved you. I love you with all my heart." As the words spill from my lips, a pain I've carried deep in my chest suddenly lifts, releasing a flood of tears that I can't restrain.

Covering my face in humiliation, I sob and repeat the words.

"I love you, Max. I'm so sorry I'm like this. You deserve better than me."

"Baby, look at me."

Max tries to peel my hands away from my face, but I'm too ashamed to face him. I'm a sad, pathetic, weak girl and not only do I cry far more often than I let on, I've been lying for two years that I'm not crazy in love with the sweetest, kindest, most handsome man I've ever met.

Am I insane? Who does these things?

Shaking my head, I try to squirm away, but he lifts me over his shoulder and marches us both towards my bedroom. I'm so distraught, I hardly notice until I land on my bed and watch him throw his jacket across the room.

"Max..." Shaken out of my stupor, I pull at my covers and try to wipe face.

Crawling over me, he unbuttons his shirt, pulling it off his shoulders as he whispers, "Say it again. Look at me, Luna. Say it again."

I hesitate. It's harder now. It means more when we make love, and this might send me over an edge I will never come back from.

"Max..." My lip quivers as I struggle to get the words past my throat.

"I love you, Luna." As his face moves towards mine, I lunge forward, taking his lips and peeling off the rest of his shirt.

"I love you. I love you, Max. I promise, I've always loved you. I loved you that first morning. I wanted to say it back so badly, but I couldn't. I don't know what's wrong with me."

I kiss him, wildly, passionately, eager to taste him after two months apart. Winding my fingers through his dark hair, I pull myself up and he glides me into his lap. Tugging at my blouse, he interrupts our kiss when he pulls it over my head, unlatching my bra and caressing my breasts while our mouths seek the other, desperate to recapture lost time.

"You're not keeping me away anymore, Luna. I won't let you." He hisses as his soft lips trail down my neck.

"I won't. I can't." I whisper as I rest my cheek against his, inhaling the scent of his cologne and soaking up his warmth. It feels so good to be in his arms again.

All I want to do is runaway with him and never look back.

Bringing his mouth to mine, he kisses me slowly, teasing me before he halts and takes my face in his hands.

"And no more telling people you can't stand me. Do you have any idea how shitty that is? Everyone knows I'm in love with you. You make me look like an idiot." He scolds and I nod.

"I won't. I'm sorry. It is shitty. *Super shitty.*"

"Then why?" He raises an eyebrow.

"The more I talk about you, the more I give myself away. I'm afraid they'll read it all over my face. I'm so sorry. You're so wonderful and I've been such an asshole." I pout and feel my eyes mist again.

Swooping in, he recaptures my lips and deepens our kiss, sating two years of unrequited love. He smothers my moans, devours my lips and nuzzles his way down my neck as I whimper with an unleashed desire that has remained dormant for far too long.

"I'm not your secret anymore, Luna." He chides as his hands travel to my breasts, gently smoothing my supple skin, before he traps them roughly in his large hands. His tender, loving caresses quickly escalate to a savage, lusty massage, as he tugs on my tight nipples and makes me whimper for more. Max knows my body. He knows every little thing that drives me wild. No one has ever come close.

"Luna, get these panties off. Now." He pushes me off his lap and unzips his pants, pointing as he instructs.

I eagerly comply. I love this Max. This is mad Max. And mad Max rules my world.

I slink them off as he watches. He could do it himself, but he wants me to submit to his command and surrender to his wishes. I have it coming. *I know I do.* When he asks for them, I toss them on his face, eager to rile him up and get things down and dirty. Smiling as he runs them down his face, he grips my waist and pushes me to the top of the bed.

"You've been such a terrible girl." He groans, as he licks my nipples and grazes his teeth against my sensitive flesh.

I tremble with lust, stuttering as I speak. "Oh no, baby. I'll be a good girl from now on."

"That's doubtful." He spreads my legs and brings up my knees, lifting my ass in the process.

Dipping his finger in my slick pussy, he shows me his wet finger. "This doesn't look like a good girl, baby. This looks like a nasty girl."

"Max! That's your fault!" I pout and blush, feigning innocence.

"It is? Then I guess I'll have to clean you up."

SIX

MAX

"Say it again." My hand travels down her slit, stopping to make lazy circles on her clit as I spread her legs wider and gather fluid on my fingers.

"I love you, baby." She moans, and watches me stick a finger in my mouth, licking it clean.

"How do I taste?"

"I think I need more." I grab her roughly, make her hold her legs open and sink my tongue in her gushing, dripping channel.

"Oh no, Max! What are you doing?" She loves playing the innocent. She knows how fucking hot it gets me.

Glancing up, I watch her twist, shuddering and aching for release, expecting me to make her come quick, like I always do.

"Play with yourself, Luna." I command, taking her hand and guiding her finger on her clit.

"Max! But you'll see me. That's so private." She bats her long lashes and bites her lip, pretending she's too embarrassed to start.

Moving her finger for her, she soon takes over on her own.

"That's it, baby. Come for me, I want to see you come."

To make the offer more enticing, I pull off my boxers and show her my hard cock. Holding it in my hand, I stroke it and gaze into those pale blue eyes.

"As soon as you come, I'll give you this." I edge closer and her eyes grow larger.

She strums her clit harder, writhing in ecstasy, reaching for my cock with her free hand but still screaming how mortified she is playing with herself in front of me.

Goddamn, she knows how to put on a show.

"You look so beautiful, baby." As I watch with bated breath, I inch closer and rub my cock on her pussy, distracting her from her goal.

Mewing and panting, she frowns at me, upset that I'm ruining her perfect rhythm, but continues her mission with such intensity, it catches her by surprise. Screaming with reckless abandon, she writhes helplessly as a second orgasm follows the first, sending her trembling body into a savage display of sexual gratification that leaves me shocked and stunned.

"Max!" She reaches for me.

"Baby! That was fucking incredible."

Her screams of pleasure quickly transform into a deep moan, as I slide my cock into her sleek pussy in one thrust. When I pull all the way out, she wraps her legs around my waist and pushes me back in, whimpering and wailing for more.

"You want more, Luna?" I slide it in, working her clit as I pull out and back in again.

She nods. "Please, fuck me Max. It's been so long." She grinds into me, shivering with need as her back arches over and over, writhing in a fit of escalating desire.

"That's your fault, Luna. You could have had this cock every day." I roll us over and make her straddle my hips. I think I'm punishing her, but she takes her cue and rides me hard.

With her beautiful tits bouncing in my face and her tight pussy clenching and squeezing my cock as she slides down without mercy or tenderness, I know the end is near.

Two months was too long. She will pay for this.

"Fuck me, Luna! Ride my cock, baby! Show me how much you missed me."

I shouldn't have challenged her. I know better.

With a reckless desire, she rides me faster and harder. Rotating her hips, she set a fierce, brutal pace, while I try to hold her steady, gasping for air, and begging her to ease up.

"Luna, slow down, I'm going to come." I grip her waist to keep her still, but she uses her ass to gyrate forward, making it worse, rubbing her clit against my skin until she gasps and falls forward, vibrating and crying as she screams my name.

"Oh God, Max! I love you!" Sealing her lips to mine, I growl and hold her tight as the shuddering ecstasy of our combined passion consumes us both.

Things are different now. I know they are.

SEVEN

LUNA

"Don't do this to me, Luna." Max struggles to pull me out from the blankets.

I lost count. We made love so many times through the storm and into the early morning, I lost count. I'm not sure that's ever happened before. We were making up for lost time and since last night was so special, he wanted to make the moment last. It wasn't a sacrifice, but the man gave me no rest. Max is sublime, a god amongst men, and far and beyond the best lover I've ever had.

He's only one of three, but the other two weren't terrible. They just weren't Max. Not just anyone can be a Max.

"That's enough. I'm exhausted, baby." I whine, making myself into a tiny ball to keep him from grabbing any erogenous zones.

"Sweetheart, I am so hard."

"But that's normal. Isn't it? Maybe you just need to use the restroom. Go try. I'll wait here." I peek over the bedsheet, but he narrows his eyes and wrenches me out.

"Get over here. I need to leave soon, and I just want to hold you." He spoons me, stabbing me in the back with his erection as he nuzzles in as tightly as possible.

"I feel like I'm being held up. That cock feels aggressive, mister." I giggle and he nibbles my shoulder, grinding his hard-on deeper.

"This cock is going to get angrier if you don't make an honest man of me. You don't think I'm going to forget about us getting married, do you?" He growls into my ear and I freeze. I knew he wouldn't hold out for much longer.

"*He* needs to mind *his* business." I look over my shoulder and smile, trying to lighten a soon-to-be awkward conversation. "He's been bossing me around all night."

He pinches my side. "Luna. Talk to me."

I sigh, exhaling deeply and clutch the big arm wrapped around my stomach.

"I'm not going to run, I promise. I love being here with you. I want you here tonight and tomorrow or I can go to you. But shouldn't we see how this goes, first? I mean, before we start talking about getting married." I reach for my pillow and ever so slightly cover my head, expecting him to reprimand me for being flaky again.

Turning me over, he brings me into his chest and kisses the top of my head. "How much time, Luna? We love each other, right?"

Covering his chest with kisses, I nod decisively. "I love you, Max. And I know this isn't sudden for you. I know I've been an incredible pain in the ass, but I need a little bit of time being your girl-friend. Do you understand?"

A pout forms as my lip trembles with fear and sadness. I don't want to lose him. "Can I have a couple of weeks before we revisit this? I'm not cutting you out. I'm not going away. I'll give you a key. But this is a lot for me."

He tilts his head and kisses my forehead. "You can have some time. But you're not pushing me away, Luna. I took video of you sleeping and I will post it all over social media if you start telling people you hate me again."

My mouth falls open in shock. "You did not!"

"I did. You were snoring. It was very unattractive." He chuckles as he jumps out of bed and makes a quick search for his discarded clothes.

"Max! It was raining. You know I have allergies." I slide out of bed, naked and reach for my panties. When he spots me, he rushes over to my side.

"Baby come on. You left me wanting." Stealing my underwear, he tries to push me back in bed.

"Maxwell Butler. You fiend. You've had your fill for one night. You'll get more tonight. I have a job interview. I need to get ready." I squirm away and rush into the bathroom.

"Interview? Where? Why?" He sounds concerned.

"My parents have threatened to cut me off. I only have a part-time job right now. I need more money." I holler as I start the shower.

"But I'll take care of you, sweetheart. You can start your own magazine, like you've always wanted." He shuffles in, sneaking into the shower before me.

I knew he'd say that. Max has so much money, he can't help himself. I grew up in privilege, but we had limitations. I'm not sure Max knows what those are. He wants to make things easy. He thinks if he gives me everything I want, every luxury imaginable, then I'll have to say yes. Because who wouldn't want to live a life of leisure with a gorgeous man? But I don't love Max for his money. *I really don't.* This man is special. His kind of money makes me nervous.

If Max was just an ordinary guy, a little school teacher, a plumber or carpenter, I think I wouldn't feel so much anxiety about being in love with him. Sure, we'd struggle, but I'd work hard, and I know we could be happy with less. Right now, there isn't a single woman in Manhattan who wouldn't love to sink her hooks into the only son and heir of Hugo Butler, especially when he's as hot as Max. Maybe one day they will. Maybe one day, when he's comfortable in my love, he'll look for someone else to chase. And by then, it'll be too late for me. By then, I won't be able to stop loving him.

"I know you don't trust me. Maybe you want me to feel desperate and destitute..."

He cuts me off. "I do not! If a new job will make you happy, I want you to be happy." He kisses me as he lathers me up.

"It's not really about happiness. I don't want to come to you from a place of desperation. I need you to know I had options and I still chose you. I owe you at least that." I make him look at me and he nods.

"Okay, baby. I hope you get that job. I mean it. I love you."

Jumping into his arms, I rain kisses on those beautiful full lips and hug him so tightly we almost fall over.

"I love you, Max. Please believe I'm trying. Let me get used to us. We won't go back to the way we were. I promise."

EIGHT

MAX

My father's been blowing up my phone all morning. He's meeting with the Forsythe's later today and I know he wants me with him. I can't go behind Luna's back now that we're working on things, but she's right. I don't trust her. *Why would I?* After two years of breaking my heart repeatedly with her indecisive bullshit, how can I believe she's changed overnight? A big part of me wants her to feel desperate and destitute.

I know. I'm an asshole. But I can't take any chances she'll go back on her word.

She's interviewing with a new lifestyle magazine today. Poor Luna. She's a great writer and she has connections. I have no doubt she'd be great at it. There's a possibility they might have wanted to hire her, but one call from my father and they agreed not to give her the job. Those idiots weren't supposed to let her get to the interview stage. That's just mean. I don't want her hopes built up just to be let down.

I hate that she's trying so hard but I'm suspicious she just wants a back-up plan in case she runs again. I can't bear it. Not again. Not after last night. I'll make it up to her. Her magazine will be bigger than this little rag. When we're married, I'll give her whatever she wants.

Not that she's agreed. No, that would be too easy. She needs to think about it longer. Two years hasn't been enough time to figure out if she loves me or not.

Rushing into my father's office, I ask his assistant if he's available.

"He's waiting for you." She buzzes me in, and I try to look as presentable as possible, in the same suit I was wearing yesterday. Maybe he won't notice.

"Dad." I avoid eye contact and creep towards a chair.

"Where the hell have you been? You weren't home. I stopped in with bagels this morning and you hadn't been there all night. Since you're wearing the same suit, I take it you got lucky." He stares at me, waiting for an answer.

"I was with Luna." I stand to grab a cup of coffee from his machine.

"Luna? Are things better? Do I still have to meet with these arrogant assholes?" Dad is acting on my behalf, but he hates people like the Forsythe's. They've been knocking him down his whole life.

I hesitate to tell him everything. I don't want to abandon the plan entirely. I promised Orson I would try to help him, but that's beyond my control. I don't want Lola to get disowned over this. She seems like a sweet girl. Castor may have been a cad in the past, but if he's cleaned up his act and loves Lola, then I don't think Orson should keep trying. It doesn't matter anyway. His father will turn the screws on his own friend just because his son doesn't get his way.

And how am I any different? No, Luna and I love each other. I wouldn't be pressuring her to marry me if I believed she was in love with another man. And besides, Dad isn't their friend.

That's right. Justify your bullshit.

"So, what are we doing then?" Dad leans back in his chair and glares at me.

"I'm investing a lot of fucking money in these people's hotels. They're good hotels, but hotels have never been my thing. All my shares will be signed over to you when you marry this girl and what you do after that, I don't care. Cut these bastards out if you want. They're dicks for using their daughters to help recover their losses. He was the idiot who trusted that ridiculous hedge fund manager. I could tell that guy was a crook the minute I saw him." Dad rants and I listen, trying to figure out my plan.

"Their younger daughter, Lola, is marrying Castor Dewitt. They're in love. I think Elmer Forsythe tried to appease Ken Dewitt by offering up Luna, knowing Luna would never agree. But she and Castor conspired to have him ask Lola instead. He's been crazy about her for years and she's loved him since she was a little girl. Now, they're getting married and blissfully in love. Orson still wants to marry a girl who clearly wants to marry someone else." I throw up my arms in confusion.

"Fuck Orson De Clare and his pompous-ass father. Theo is worse than Elmer! They're trying to corner this poor girl into marrying Orson, and I don't want you doing the same. I'm only going along with this because you swear she loves you. If she doesn't, don't do this. It's far too expensive and the toll will be much higher when she divorces your ass and takes your children."

"No, Luna loves me. We talked about it, last night. She won't agree to marry me, yet. But she's inching her way there. Let's just meet with the Forsythe's and see what they have to say. I'm marrying Luna either way. Maybe this is a good investment for the future. This will be our children's legacy." As I speak, I feel my father's eyes on me. I feel his judgment and I'm perfectly aware of how insane I sound.

He narrows his eyes. "Maybe, I've indulged you too much. Am I enabling this psychosis?"

"Perhaps."

Reaching for his jacket, he takes the opportunity to mock me.

"Do yourself a favor, son. Don't just have one child. Spread the love around. You get far too invested when you only have one."

"Oh, leave me alone."

NINE

LUNA

For the life of me, I do not understand what Lola sees in Castor Dewitt, but I won't deny she looks happier than I've ever seen her. Listening to her talk about her wedding and all the plans she's making for her new life in France hurts my heart, but only because I'll miss her, not because I'm jealous. I want her to be happy and deep down, I want to feel like that too.

What's missing? It can't still be him. It's been so long.

If Castor is good to Lola and makes her happy, then he can't be all that bad, but I'm not crazy about the way he's simply absconded with her over the past week. Since their engagement, I've hardly seen her. I planned this breakfast two days ago, hoping to have some quiet time with my baby sister, but apparently, he can't keep away.

Halfway through my second mimosa, Castor comes charging in with something on his mind.

"Luna, when was the last time you spoke to Max Butler?" He stares at me, and piques Lola's curiosity.

"Max Butler? Luna? Are they still trying to set you up with him?" Lola leans in, concerned I'm being bullied into marrying a man whose handprint is still etched brightly on my ass after we played a particularly over the top version of Daddy's bad girl last night.

"Why?" I chirp.

Oh damn, I just gave myself away. But I can't even pretend to be angry at him. Even when he's a huge pervert, he always makes me feel like a princess.

"Were they trying to arrange you to him?" Castor's so nosy. Before I can answer, Lola speaks for me.

"They were. Our parents had no intention of letting her say yes to you. Mother said Max Butler wanted to marry her. His father plans to invest a ton of money in Daddy's hotels. Have you seen him, Luna?"

"Just a little." There's no sense in denying it. All this will come out soon enough.

"What the hell does that mean? You said you hate him." Lola pounds the table and Castor knits his brow.

There's no easy answer, but I promised Max I wouldn't tell people I hate him.

"I have needs and you've been gone all week. Max has been texting like crazy. That night it stormed, he came over to keep me company and then came back the night after that. But one more night and I put an end to it, I swear." I lie. He's been by every night and some afternoons. We're making dinner later tonight.

Oh, crap! I need to pick up some dessert before I go home. He wants something with whipped cream.

"Luna! You said you hate him! How do you get hot and bothered for someone you hate?"

I don't need this judgement.

"I never said I hated having sex with him. I don't know why he wants to marry me, but he does. His father is helping him make it happen. He doesn't give a fuck about Orson except they had a deal to try to make this happen. I guess they're friends."

After the two play twenty questions, Castor scolds me and leaves on his merry way. I'm annoyed, but not just at him. Max doesn't trust me. He's made sure my parents don't pester me. He promised to give me room to think, but he's taking precautions. Although I can't blame him, I wish he'd have a little faith in me.

I really am trying this time.

As for my parents, they can't help themselves. It's far more important that I marry Max, but they're punishing Lola to be vindictive little shits. It's insurance. Torturing her makes me pliable. They know I'll do anything to protect her.

And they know better than to place their fragile eggs in the Luna basket.

I don't want Lola paying the price for my indecisiveness or Max's persistence. What the hell do I do? I'm not ready to jump into marriage yet. This is a huge deal and love isn't always enough to make things work.

"Sorry about that, Castor can be very protective. He hates the way Mother and Daddy are behaving towards me." Lola apologizes for Castor.

"I am, too, sweetie. I don't want them acting this way. I'm sorry if I'm making things worse for you. I'll talk to Max." I call the waitress, avoiding eye contact with my sister. She's staring at me, trying to determine how much I'm holding back, but I'm not ready to divulge anymore. Once I tell Lola. It's real.

That's the way it is with sisters.

TEN

MAX

Something is wrong. I can feel it. Luna is giving me what I want. She's talking more and more about getting married and making a life together, but there's something missing. I can see it in her eyes.

My girl is terrified, and she won't tell me why.

Lying in bed, she pulls out a book and reads. I could easily talk her into having sex, but I wish she'd talk to me instead. I wish she'd tell me what's holding her back. Every time I hear news about Castor and Lola, I feel like punching that bastard for having it so easy. He came out of nowhere, professed his love for Lola and she flew into his arms without any hesitation. They were engaged by midday and she was wearing his ring before *Cartier* closed that evening.

It's infuriating!

Luna won't go ring shopping, not even to look or give me hints. She says it's bad luck. *She's so full of shit.* I don't want to pressure her, but it's been over two weeks and although she's talking about it, she won't give me a definitive answer.

Dragging her into my arms, I rest my chin on her shoulder. "Talk to me, Luna."

She sighs. "Why don't you talk to me, Max?"

My heart sinks. I'm in trouble. But for what? I've done so much behind her back, where the hell do I begin?

"About what, sweetheart?" I need clarification before I get myself in more trouble.

"Why are you letting Orson, Theo and your Dad torture my sister? Did you speak with my parents?" She bows her head. She knows the answer. If I lie, it could cost me everything.

"I did. I'm sorry. That was a while ago. I asked them not to bother you. I know nothing about Lola."

I really don't.

"That's Theo De Clare, I promise. And probably your parents."

"You don't trust me. You wanted insurance, right?" She weaves her fingers through my hair and pulls me closer, resting her head on mine.

"Sweetheart, I love you. Why don't you tell me what's wrong? Is there someone else?" My heart aches asking the question. I know there's no one now. I keep tabs on her all day. But maybe there's someone in her past.

She shakes her head. "No. I'm just scared things will change."

"But they will change. They'll get better. Let me love you, Luna. I mean that. Let me love all of you. Whatever you're hiding, whatever wounds you won't let me see, I love those too. As crazy as you make me, I love you. I don't want to change you. I just don't want you to be scared anymore." I hold her tighter, fearful I've said too much, but when she exhales and falls into my chest, I confess more.

"Your parents are cutting you off Luna. They've stopped paying for your lease and your accounts will close when Lola marries. They don't want you to know because they want it to be a surprise. If you learn about it after the fact, you'll be forced to marry me to keep from being homeless and poor." I kiss her cheek, but she tenses.

Sliding away from me, she reaches for her robe and pulls her hair up. "Max, can you leave?"

"Luna! I told you that to warn you, not to pressure you more." My pulse quickens and I fly out of bed and rush over to calm her.

Did I just fucking ruin everything?

Holding her hand up, she stops me and strokes my chest to soothe me.

"I'm mad at you, but I'm not furious. I'm not sending you away because I want to end things, I promise." She mumbles, sadly.

"It feels that way." I frown, reach for my boxers and sit on the bed, exasperated.

"Maxwell Butler, you are not the only man I could marry if I found myself homeless! I don't mean to brag, but there are other men who could keep me living nicely. I am not marrying you for your money!" She sneers with fury and pushes me back on the bed.

"What the hell does that mean?" I pant with anxiety as my heart thumps loudly in my chest.

"It means... I love you. I know what you do. I know you keep an eye on me. I know you own my building and could easily extend my lease if you wanted. I know you don't trust me, and I feel so bad about everything, I've chosen not to be upset by it."

Her words break my heart. I don't want to break her spirit. Her spirit is what I love most about her.

"So, when can I see you?" I reach for her hand and kiss it, using mind powers I don't have to will her to forgive me.

"Give me a few days to think about everything." She rushes into her closet.

"Luna! No! Three days! What do you have to think about? You said two weeks, and it's been almost four." I chase after her.

"Fine. Three? I was thinking four or five, but I'll shrink it to two since you're going to be a baby. Two days. Can you give me two days?"

I nod, begrudgingly. "Fine. I'm making dinner plans for us in two days, Luna. Either you have an answer, or you spill your guts about why you don't have an answer."

"Yes, yes. Stop being so bossy! It's still me under all this love, you know." She pushes me aside and searches for her shoes.

"Where are you going, it's almost 10:00?" I eye her suspiciously, still annoyed by her earlier comment referencing other men she could marry.

"I am going to pay Mrs. Katherine Forsythe a visit and let her have a piece of my mind!" She points her finger in the air and marches into the bathroom to brush her hair.

"Your Mom? What about your Dad?"

"He'll get some, too. But my beef is with her. It's always been with her!"

"Do you need a ride?" I grab my jeans and dress as quickly as possible.

"Yes, come on. It's getting late."

ELEVEN

LUNA

I'm not sure why I waste my time with that woman. She knows nothing but her own suffering. All she did was get me frazzled and because of her, I probably blew my sixth interview the following morning.

I'm seeing Max tonight. I don't want to say no. I'm not sure if I'm ready to say yes, but I'm sure as shit not ready to tell him everything. After all this time, it seems dumb and juvenile. I feel like a crazy person and no one wants to marry a crazy person.

Maybe I'm worried people will find out the truth? Am I ashamed?

No. I tried to find him. I was so young, and I tried. She wouldn't help me, but I tried. Then, he was gone. What if I end up like him? I can't think about this now. I need to plan for tonight. I haven't seen Max in two days and it will take him five minutes to get these panties off. I know him. One wink and they'll go flying.

Stay strong, Luna. He's just a man.

Thinking about a ridiculous idea my friend Geneva, gave me, I barge into Lola's room. She's packing, and the sight hurts my heart. She'll be so far. Why did I help Castor? He hardly knows her! He probably doesn't even know that onions make her gag, or that she cries hysterically every time that ASPCA commercial comes on.

"Lola, do you have a tampon?" I mumble the words, knowing full well she knows my cycle and will be on to me in seconds.

"No, sorry. But you're not due yet, why do you need one?" She gazes at me, eyes full of suspicion.

I explain Geneva's plan. It's asinine, but she thinks I should pack my purse full of tampons and let one fly out during dinner to steer Max from trying to spend the night. It's only good in theory. Max couldn't care less and I'm pretty sure that creeper knows my cycle like clockwork.

Lola scoffs, but her demeanor quickly transforms and as she struts into the closet, she asks me the question I've been dreading.

"Are you in love with him?"

Rats. Not this. Not now.

I deny it. It's only about the sex. I'm not in love. I'm emphatic, but I can tell she doesn't believe a damn word I'm saying. It's pathetic. My act might be more convincing if the few tears that I've been fighting all evening hadn't finally made their appearance and invited a thousand more friends. Blubbering hysterically, I shake my head in shame and disgrace, swearing I don't know how I feel.

Lola pries but she isn't persistent. She wants to know, but it's not in her nature to force it out of me. Instead, she hugs me and lets me cry. It's embarrassing. I shouldn't burden her with my problems, but other than Max, she's the person I love most in the world. If anyone would understand, she would. But she doesn't deserve to hear it first. He does.

In my state of despair, I think.

For one moment, I think about Max and our future. The world disappears and all I see is his face.

I know what to do.

Lola chases me into my room, but my mind is made up. I love him. I can't run away from love forever. I can help set things right for Lola and maybe, just maybe, be happy too.

TWELVE

MAX

I'm ready. I know she's going to have a perfectly logical argument, memorized down to the smallest detail. She'll leave nothing to chance. I've been writing notes all day. Would you believe I pulled out a thesaurus several times? That's how serious I am about laying out my argument for marriage. *A fucking thesaurus!*

I graduated Columbia Law. I don't think I need to prove my intelligence, but that girl gets me so tied up in knots, I constantly feel like I need to make an impression. If I could have brought my computer without looking like a complete idiot, I would have rented the private room and set up a presentation.

Luna is not catching me by surprise. Just to round things up, I bought a ring. I know her taste by now and if she doesn't like it, we can exchange it for another. I'm not sensitive. The important thing is that she's happy. She'll be wearing it for a long time.

Have you had enough? You sound insane.

I'm not sure why I had to meet her here. This feels like a bad sign.

I'm not above pulling out all my money from her parents' hotels and letting everything flush down the toilet. I'll save the house in Croton. It has sentimental value.

Goddammit, Luna. Don't do this.

By the time she arrives I'm so full of anxious energy, I've eaten half our basket of bread. She's not late, I arrived early. Hiding my notes before she reaches the table, I stand to help her into her seat. She looks beautiful, but I can tell she's been crying. This doesn't feel right. I know she's going to dump me. I can feel it. Why would she dress so nice just to dump me?

"You look handsome." She smiles and pulls her napkin out, fixing it on her lap.

"You look beautiful, sweetheart. But why do you look sad?" I take her hand in mine and she squeezes it tightly. My heart skips. I fear she's about to say something terrible.

"Lola was packing when I left. It was a sad sight. I'll miss her." She sighs and gazes at me, working up the nerve to say something.

"Max..." She whispers under her breath and I cut her off. I can't bear it.

"Luna, I know what you're going to say...and I know I've been pressuring you, but you mean the world to me and---" She squeezes my hand so tight, I stop abruptly.

"You're ruining my moment, Max. You don't know what I'm going to say." She frowns and places a finger across her lips to shut me up.

"I wanted to say that I hope you and I have more than one baby. I don't like that you grew up by yourself. Having a sister is one of the best parts of my life and I want that for our children."

I freeze. I feel my heart soaring, but my brain is frozen, unable to do anything but focus on those pale blue eyes. Luna is saying yes. *I think my Luna is saying yes.*

"Luna…" I swallow hard, struggling to be eloquent, and then simply fighting to speak the words. "Are you marrying me?"

She nods and a big smile crosses that gorgeous face. "Yeah, I am. Is your offer still good, Mr. Butler?"

"Hell, yes. I love you, Luna." I stand, and pull her up, hugging her tighter than I've ever hugged her before. My baby is marrying me.

Luna Forsythe is marrying me.

"I love you, Max. Can we marry in Croton? At the end of summer or early Fall?" She rests her head on my chest and wraps her arms around my waist.

"Sure, sweetheart. Whatever you want. Wherever you want." I kiss the top of her head and for the first time in two years I feel I can breathe again. I waited for this moment for so long, always knowing it was meant to be, but always fearing it would never come.

Desperate to be alone, we try to get through dinner as quickly as we can. We have plans to make and people to call, but first, there are some panties that need removing.

THIRTEEN

LUNA

"**M**ax! Wait until we get inside!" Kissing the back of my neck, his hands caress every curve. He moves down my breasts, my waist, smoothing my ass, before sliding in front and cupping my pussy roughly, claiming it as he growls into my ear.

Pushing open the door, we almost fall in together as we make a race for his bedroom. We rarely stay at his place, but with Lola packing, I don't want to take any chances she'll hear my nasty screams of praise. Tonight, is special and I have a feeling a variety of Maxwells will make an appearance.

When we reach the bedroom, he backs away and slowly undresses, giving me a naughty striptease that holds me so enraptured I stand stunned, staring at every gorgeous muscle instead of working to remove my own attire.

"Luna, why are you still wearing panties?" He barks and I snap to attention.

"Sorry, sir. I'm on it." I giggle as I slide out of my dress, toss my bra on the floor and throw my panties at his feet.

Taking me into his arms, he lifts me gently and carries me on to his huge bed.

He wastes no time getting nasty. Without a word, he spreads my legs and I gasp when he buries his face in my soaked lips. Driving his tongue deep, I whimper and shudder while he strums my clit, fingering me until my walls tighten and my hips pump against his face. I writhe aimlessly, wailing his name in the throes of passion, screaming praise for his talents and calling to the heavens for mercy when I'm struck blind with wave after wave of unimaginable pleasure, twisting my body into a fitful frenzy of ecstasy that shocks me speechless.

I try to reach for his cock, hungry to feel it in my mouth, but he's too eager to come. Flipping me over on my knees, he thrusts his hard cock deep inside me, giving it all, stretching me open and then demanding more.

"Come get it, baby." Gripping my hips, he pulls me back, making me fuck him and I eagerly give him what he wants.

"Like this?" I slam into him, surprising him with my enthusiasm and forcing a low grunt to escape his mouth.

"Just like that, angel. Give it to me. Fuck me, Luna. Come get this cock." He spanks me, making me tremble with a euphoric thrill.

I give him what he wants, setting a brutal pace, but when he wants to slow down, I find it hard to stop. Giving me no choice, he teases me, withholding my prize, until I go crazy, pushing and grinding into his dick with a reckless desire that stuns him into submission. Turning the tables, he pushes me forward and thrusts harder, holding me tightly while I gasp for air, claw the sheets and wail until our bodies collapse in a state of sweet agony, overwhelmed by one climax after another.

Lying exhausted, I relax into his arms and kiss his huge chest, completely enthralled with this beautiful man.

"Do you like your ring baby?"

"More than anything." I lift my hand and gaze at it for the tenth time, letting it shimmer in the light above. "I can't believe you picked something so perfect for me. It's a little big, but I'll let that slide."

I seal my lips to his, caress his perfectly chiseled face and gaze into those beautiful green eyes. I'm going to marry Max Butler. I'm blissfully in love and can't imagine my life without him.

How strange.

FOURTEEN

MAX

We marry tomorrow morning. Lola and Castor arrived from France this morning and Luna's been catching up with her sister most of the day. Her parents are here, but she's not letting her father walk her down the aisle. Since he didn't walk Lola, she feels there needs to be a show of sisterly solidarity. I don't care. I don't care if anyone is here, besides my parents and Luna.

But for Luna's sake, I'm glad Lola is here. She's missed her terribly.

Being in Croton together again feels like coming home. Our first day back, we walked to the coffee shop, went for a boat ride and spent the day walking all over this small town. Luna loves it here and I get why she wanted to marry in Autumn. It's a perfect setting.

We're getting married at her grandparent's estate, which we now own, and Luna has spent the last few weekends coming here to help renovate it for the wedding. She's taken every little part of the planning to heart and even talks about starting our family within the year, now that Lola is expecting.

But I know something is wrong.

I can feel it in my bones.

I know my Luna. There's something behind those eyes. Panic. Something is bubbling up, but she won't talk about it. All she wants to do is bury it with work or plans for our future.

We're not sleeping together tonight. She's staying in the house and I'm staying at the hotel. I can't complain. She didn't make me go through a strange abstinence period, but she requested one night apart, since we aren't supposed to see one another the day of the wedding. One night won't kill me. We have the rest of our lives.

I sneak to the house before midnight to say goodnight and she creeps out on to the porch in a small white nightgown that makes her look like a teenager.

She looks adorable.

"I knew you'd come." She jumps into my arms and I exhale in relief. I'm terrified she'll disappear. I won't be fully content until we're married. It's pathetic, I know.

"I had to say goodnight to my girl." I close my mouth over hers and kiss my beautiful Luna for one last time before she's my wife. Licking her full, pink lips, I force her mouth open with my tongue and melt into her, tasting her, letting the entire world disappear in our kiss.

One more sleep and she's mine forever.

FIFTEEN

LUNA

"How are you doing, champ?" Lola gazes at me through the mirror, smiling silly and giving me a thumbs up.

"Stop that. I'm getting ready." I finish applying some lipstick and she hands me the gloss I have standing by. She's trying to be helpful, but I know what she's doing. She thinks I'm scared.

"That's a gorgeous dress and look at those shoes! I wish I had gone more non-traditional. But you were always the stylish one." She pulls up a chair and runs her hand across the fabric of my skirt.

"Lola, you're freaking me out."

"Luna! I know you're scared. I see it in your eyes. Talk to me." She grabs my shoulders and makes me face her.

I shake my head in frustration. "I am not. I'm excited."

"Luna, I'm a married woman now. I can sense these things. I've been where you've been, and I can see panic coming out of every pore." She smirks.

"You have got to be kidding me."

"Okay, the married part is bullshit. I've just always wanted to say that. But as your sister, I know you. Tell me you're okay." She leans in and places her head next to mine.

"I'm okay." I knit my brows.

"You're lying. But it's okay, I'm here to help." She rushes to her purse and breaks out a small vial of essential oils, waving it over my face. As she does, our mother walks in uninvited and unannounced.

"Lola! Get that away from her. You're going to spill it on her dress." She crosses the bedroom to my vanity and tries to do her best impression of a loving mother.

"Mother, you should leave. I don't want you upsetting me before the wedding." I scowl and try to worm my way out of her grasp.

"Nonsense, what do you have to be upset about? You're marrying a handsome man, one of the richest in New York and he seems to love you. Love might not always last, but you're young and beautiful. I'm sure you'll have your husband's undivided attention for years to come."

Lola gasps, and watches me fall back into my chair. Taking my mother by the arm, she calls out to Castor who's waiting nearby. "Get her out of here! Take her to my father and don't let her anywhere near Luna again."

Returning to my side, she kneels and takes my hand. "Don't listen to her. Max loves you. And you love him, Luna. I know you do. I knew you loved him even when you lied right to my face and said you hated him. Because I'm your sister and it's my job to know." She smiles and hugs me.

"Do you know about my Dad?" I stare at her and my heart sinks saying the words.

Her eyes fill with tears and she nods slowly. "Yeah. I know."

"I don't want to end up like him, Lola." I gasp, clutch my heart and struggle to hold in my tears.

"Luna! Why would you? You never met him." She holds my hand and I suspect she's trying to keep me from leaving. As I march around the room, looking for my purse, she keeps holding on, begging me to talk to her.

"I met him, Lola. I met him when I was five. I went looking for him when I got older." Wiping my tears, I feel the start of a panic attack. I don't know what to do, but I have to leave. I need to get out of the house.

"Lola, I'll be back. I won't go far." I wrench out of her grasp and rush down the stairs. Taking the back hallway, I sprint towards the backdoor and run towards the cars.

Weaving through the front yard, I march down the road and head towards our limo. The driver works for Max, but maybe he'll take me for a ride. I don't know what I'm doing. I don't want to leave for good, I just need to think.

Too hysterical to hear the footsteps running behind me, I jump into the backseat and almost scream when Max jumps into the other side.

"Where the hell are you going?" He looks enraged, but when he sees my red, swollen, tear-stained face, his expression lightens.

"I'm not leaving you. I just needed air." I cry into my hands, ashamed of myself and afraid to admit the truth.

"In a limo? You were getting air in a limo? For fuck's sake Luna, were you leaving me at the altar?" His teeth clench as he speaks.

"No. I don't think so. I would have gone back."

"You think?" When my tears grow heavier, he stops berating me and pulls me closer. "What happened with your mother? Lola said she upset you."

Sniffling and wiping my face, I summon the courage to tell him what I've wanted to tell him for two years. Choking on every word, I tell him why I am the way I am.

"Max... I don't belong to my father." I breathe deeply, struggling to say the words.

"What?" He looks confused.

"I don't. He doesn't know. I found out when I was five-years-old because my real father came looking for me and my mother at the house. He was young, younger than my Dad, probably my mother's age, but he was poor. She met him in college. I have his eyes. He had blonde hair and pale blue eyes. His name was David, and he loved my mother. I heard him begging her, reminding her of all the promises she made him, and she told him she didn't love him anymore." I stop to catch my breath as Max continues to listen.

"He came by every day while my father worked, wanting to see her and she'd send him away or call the police. When I was thirteen, I went looking for him, but he'd been gone for years."

Crying without restraint, I shake as grief overwhelms me. "My aunt, his younger sister, told me he died of an overdose, but she said he'd been dead for years. She said he died of a broken heart the year he lost my mother. She'd been the love of his life and he never understood how someone who loved him so much could just stop. Like, he was nothing."

Max is speechless, so instead of speaking, he brings me into his lap and wipes my tears.

"I'm not leaving you. I'm not her. I'm just afraid I'm him. I'm scared you've only loved me because I was hard to catch and now that we're married, you'll find someone else to chase. Max, I don't want to die of a broken heart. And if you ever leave me, I will." I rest my head on his shoulder and sob uncontrollably.

"Sweetheart, if you leave me, I will too." He kisses my salty cheek and rocks me gently. "We're stuck with one another. I can't live without you, Luna Forsythe. I will die a lonely, broken, old man if I don't have you by my side."

"But how can we be sure?" I hug him, loving him more by the second.

"Because you're my person."

My heart melts at the memory of that word. "Did Castor tell you to say that?" I look at him sharply.

"Castor? I can't stand him. You think I take love advice from Castor? You're my person Luna Forsythe. And you better believe I'm yours."

"You are, Maxwell Butler."

"Now, will you please cut your shit and marry me already?" He runs his finger down my nose."

I nod. "Are you sure?"

"Get out of the car, Luna. You're stuck with me. You'll never shake me loose."

SIXTEEN

·   ·   ·

EPILOGUE- TWO YEARS LATER

MAX

It was a lovely wedding. Everyone talks about it. Luna and I had so much fun, we hardly noticed anyone else was there. By the time all the guests were gone, it was just her and I, dancing alone on the dance floor, singing to one another and having the time of our lives.

After we left for our honeymoon, my father informed the Forsythe's that we would be taking over their hotels and buying them out for good. We didn't give them a good deal. Luna insisted we be as unfair as possible.

Maybe the feeling of desperation and destitution would help them make better decisions. *Her words.*

I feel bad she's not close to her parents anymore, but Dad was right. They were using their daughters to make up for their terrible financial choices. Fortunately, Luna and Lola got lucky the arrangements worked out in their favor.

Castor and Lola are happier than ever, living in Paris with one daughter and another on the way. We've gone to visit them a few times and we'll be back again next month. It makes Luna happy to see her younger sister and whatever makes her happy, makes me happy. Besides, Castor's finally grown on me. He wasn't so bad after all. He loves Lola the way I love Luna, but of course, *Lola is no Luna.*

Life with my girl is better than I ever dreamed. We planned to wait a year to start our family, but we were pleasantly surprised when we found out we were expecting three months after our wedding. Our daughter, Amelia was born shortly after our first anniversary. My parents were thrilled. They'd always wanted a daughter and Amelia is the next best thing. We plan to try for more soon. But for now, I like it just the three of us.

Just me and my two girls.

SEVENTEEN

EPILOGUE- TEN YEARS LATER

"You're looking mighty fine, young lady." Max smiles and extends his hand.

I adjust my pink sundress, the same one I wore twelve years ago, when we met here in Croton. It fits, but after three babies, it's a little tight on the tits.

"Thank you, kind sir." I chuckle and let him help me into the small row boat.

With his powerful arms on display, I sit back and watch with delight, letting him enjoy the view of my long legs peeking out from underneath my dress.

We spend most of our time in the city. Between Max's work and my magazine, which I named *Amelia* after our first born, we work long hours Monday through Friday, but weekends are for us and for our family.

Two years after Amelia, our son Ian was born, followed by Lora two years after him. Our youngest is five and we've decided we're done. We could have more. I'm only thirty-four and Max turns forty later this year, but we're enjoying our time being bad again. After so many years of having to stifle our lovemaking for fear we'd wake a baby, I've welcomed the return of my good friend, *Mad Max.*

And as always, Mad Max rules my world.

"Luna." Max calls to me as he rows.

"Yes, sweetheart?"

"Why don't you do me a favor and get those panties off." He grins, daring me.

First clutching my chest in feigned offense, I lift my dress and show him my surprise. "Oh no, I think I forgot to put them on today."

Max's eyes grow wide as his mouth salivates with lust. Lunging across the boat, he lifts my skirt and slides down between my legs. Pushing my knees to my shoulders, he sinks his mouth deep in my pussy. He feasts ravenously, like a starving man as I watch helplessly, holding in my screams for fear I'll draw attention to our boat. When he penetrates me with his fingers, I squeal in a frenzy of lust, panting and moaning, begging for cock as he struggles to unleash it from his pants.

"I love you, Max!"

"Oh, baby, I love you so much." Sliding it in, I tremble as he splits me open, thrusting deep with passionate strokes as we both build a rhythm, panting, howling, savoring every moment we have alone to let our love consume us. When I feel myself tumbling towards my release, I grind down, rocking my hips into his, taking his cock as far as it will go and not feeling how much our rocking is shaking the boat until it flips over and takes us with it.

For heaven's sake.

We have to laugh. Thankfully we're mostly dressed, and it's a quick walk back to the house. But in typical fashion, the minute we walk in, soaking wet, we are surrounded by three screaming children who all want to know why we went swimming with our clothes on.

Almost in unison, we both reply, "Just go to your rooms."

Late at night, after everyone is fed and put to bed, Max and I lie awake, holding each other, and thinking about the two years we spent apart.

"I'm so sorry, I kept you away. I could have lost you." I sigh with regret.

"Sweetheart, you would have never lost me. You're my girl and I'll never leave my girl." He kisses my forehead and hugs me.

"Now, answer me this." He asks in a stern voice.

"What?"

"Why the hell do you still have your panties on?"

"Sorry, sir. They're coming off."

The End

ABOUT THE AUTHOR

Matilda loves many things---her husband, dachshunds, cats, the two terrible Chihuahuas who live with her, Paris, New York, a few select friends and family, Nutella, books, lots and lots of books, and writing sweet, steamy romance for nerdy girls-- because that's who I am.

If you like your romances steamy but sweet. Sexy, but on the shorter side. With smart and sassy heroines who fall for soulful Alphas- then you might like my books.

I write A LOT of OMYW, cause that's just my bag. But no matter what kind of story it is, my ladies are always adored and my endings are always HEA.

Please head to my blog to learn what's in the final stages and will be coming out soon!

ALSO BY MATILDA MARTEL

Filthy Love

Bella Hamilton is on a mission. Her best friend, Ava, is about to marry, and her surprise nuptials have thrown Bella's long-scheduled BFF plans for marriage and babies out of whack.

Never fear, Bella has a plan. She always has a plan. An interview with a young, hot billionaire is the golden opportunity she needs. And since she has no experience with men, she plans to use everything she's learned from years of reading romance novels to lure him into her web.

What on earth could go wrong?

Jude McCormick is nothing like his older brother. He doesn't believe in marriage. He doesn't yearn for a family. He goes from woman to woman and the only thing he longs for is escaping the yoke of his family's legacy.

But then he meets Bella. He's instantly attracted, but she dismisses him. He tries to flirt, but she reacts with disgust. She drives him crazy with lust, but she won't give him the time of day.

At the end of his rope, he's forced to take a harder look and the more he learns about this strange girl, the faster he falls in love.

Dirty, filthy love.

If you've ever wondered what it might be like if your significant other took cues from your favorite book boyfriends—you might like this novella!

Filthy Love is book two of a standalone series. This is an insta-love steamy romantic comedy and as always, this book contains sexy times, a happily ever after and no cheating!

Filthy Rich

Declan McCormick is filthy rich. He's gotten everything he ever wanted, but always wanted the wrong things. At thirty-eight, he's single, works seventy hours a week and comes home to an empty house every night.

Something needs to change.

Ava Jameson has come to New York to finish school. With rich parents, she's gotten everything she ever wanted, except their time. But she swears to do things differently. She has big dreams and one of those dreams is building a better family than her own.

When their paths cross, sparks fly. Declan charges full speed ahead but soon discovers the love of his life isn't so easily impressed and isn't interested in being the heroine of her own billionaire romance.

This is a short, sweet and steamy, insta-love contemporary, older man younger woman, billionaire romance novella with two people who quickly learn the best things in life never have a price tag. Enjoy!

Play Right

Ajax Easton is a Tony Award-winning playwright used to getting his way. The playwright rules supreme on the Broadway stage and his latest play *The End of Love* is set to be another hit.

Georgia Madrid is one of the hottest actresses in Hollywood. She's just won an Oscar but doesn't believe she's taken seriously. Her manager recommends the theater and specifically Ajax's play.

Georgia's not interested. She hates the theater, but she fears becoming overplayed in Hollywood.

Ajax is a theater snob and doesn't think a screen actress is right for the role, except Georgia is his muse. He's harbored a secret crush on her for years and the prospect of meeting her pushes him to agree.

Big personalities overrule mutual attraction. Sparks combust into fireworks and lovers become enemies before they realize they couldn't be a more perfect fit.

This is a steamy contemporary insta-love romantic comedy with an older playwright and his younger leading lady who fall madly in love but keep fumbling their way to their happily ever after.

Shut Up & Kiss Me

Byron Wolff and Tabitha Devine are the best of friends.

They're also secretly in love.

Byron is desperate to be with his Tabby, but he's afraid his crazy, needy side will scare her away and ruin the only healthy relationship he's ever had.

In the meantime, he continuously meddles in every date and relationship she has, fearing someone else will take her away before he works up the courage to tell her how he feels.

Tabitha is lovesick over Byron, but after three years of waiting for him to take things to another level, she fears he'll never see her as anything more than a friend--- and her patience is running thin.

When her new boss sees right through Byron, he decides to light a fire under Byron's behind--- scaring him to dive off the cliff and chase his true love.

This is a friends to lovers steamy romantic comedy about two best friends who need to shut up and finally say I love you. As always there's no cheating and a guaranteed, happily ever after.

Maestro

Music enslaves the Maestro, Passion liberates the Muse

Marek Misiak is a composer and maestro of one of the most prominent orchestras in the country. Music is his life. His only love. But his phantom muse has abandoned him. Nothing inspires him. He's chased perfection his whole life and settled for a life of mediocrity.

Aria Romero is a prodigy, a cellist virtuoso, who hides her talent from a father still mourning the death of his cellist wife.

Music is not practical. Nothing good will come from it.

When Marek meets Aria and hears her play, he finally hears true perfection. The echoes of angels. Inspiration returns. Fate has brought them together. Two halves are whole.

Attraction is instant, love is fated, but she can't risk having her secret discovered.

Marek won't be dissuaded. Destiny will prevail. The Maestro will have his Muse.

This is an older man younger woman steamy romance, with two soul mates brought together by a love of music and passion for each other. As always, there is a guaranteed happy ending!

Lucky Man

Clever Girl

Magic Man

Agreeably Arranged

There She Goes

The Perfect Nanny

A Hostile Takeover

The Good Girl

The Pastor

The Trophy Wife

My Dad's Best Friend

My Fake Husband

Queen of Two Hearts

Closing Daddy's Deal

The Girl Next Door

And many more!

For updates on new releases click here and a free ebook, click here:
www.matildamartel.com

Made in the USA
Middletown, DE
04 February 2023

23988668R00097